SHADOW IN THE DAYLIGHT

SHADOW SEALS

KALYN COOPER

Shadow in the Daylight

KaLyn Cooper

Cover Artist: Cat Johnson

Editor: Erica Scott

ISBN978-1-970145-30-4

eBook Published by Black Swan Publishing

ABOUT THIS BOOK

He was done with missions...but Charley wasn't done with him.

After he left the Navy, stripped of his SEAL Trident and his pride, Andrew did a quick covert job for Charley before parting ways. As the Security Officer aboard a cruise ship, he invited several SEAL friends to travel as his guests through the Panama Canal. He never imagined he'd need his highly trained skills for another of Charley's missions in the middle of the cruise.

Kendra had worked her way up the male-dominated bridge crew, first in the U.S. Navy then for Monarch Cruise Lines, to Staff Captain, second in command of a huge cruise ship. Her crew was well trained and respectful...except for the too sexy, bossy Security Officer who reported directly to her. After succumbing to him, she discovers she enjoys their life together.

When all hell breaks loose, and Charley needs both of them for her next mission, will Kendra be able to keep him in her life with all the odds stacked against them?

A LETTER TO READERS

Dear Reader,

Thank you so much for purchasing **Shadow in the Daylight**, the next novel in the multi-author **Shadow SEALs Series**.

Shadow in the Daylight runs parallel to **Shadow in the Darkness** by Becca Jameson, next book in this series. What that means, is that both books follow the exact same timeline. The heroes and heroines make appearances in both books. Although both books are complete romance novels—each with a happy ending and can be read as a standalone—you may wish to read both books to fully understand the complexities of the characters.

This book has many genres including; contemporary, military, romantic suspense, and action adventure.

At the end of *Shadow in the Daylight* you will find a sneak peek at *Shadow in the Darkness* by Becca Jameson.

I hope you enjoy reading *Shadow in the Daylight* and buy the other books in the **Shadow SEAL series**. For your convenience, there's a complete list and links at the end of this book.

I hope you enjoy *Shadow in the Daylight.*

Always,

KaLyn Cooper

For the latest on works in progress and future releases, check out **KaLyn Cooper's website**

   www.KaLynCooper.com   https:// kalyncooper.com/

Follow **KaLyn Cooper on Facebook** for promotions and giveaways https://www.face book.com/KaLynCooper1Author/

Sign up for exclusive promotions and special offers only available in **KaLyn's newsletter** http://www.kalyncooper.com/newsletter.html

DEDICATION

I dedicate this book to those who have had career choices taken from them, then found equally satisfying second careers, or third, or fourth.

ACKNOWLEDGMENTS

Every book I write requires my awesome team to get it into your hands and *Shadow in the Daylight* was no different.

My sincere thanks to my writing partner, Becca Jamison. Because our books run parallel once again, we had to work together closely, which isn't easy for two very different writers. You wouldn't believe the length she went in order to write her book!

My special thanks to suspense writer (and occasional lunch & travel partner) Rachel Rivers for her brainstorming sessions. As pantzers, we don't plot out a story, we just let it happen, but when it doesn't "happen" we need help from our friends to dig the right idea out of our brains. Lunch is good, too.

I'd like to thank the members of the Black Swan Book Club for their constant support!

I cannot thank my new editor, Erica Scott, enough for her patience, understanding of both plots (mine and Becca's) and speedy services.

A huge thank you to my publicist, Michelle Duke, and my personal assistant, Charlotte Oliver, for everything you do for me.

Thank you to my wonderful husband for sharing his military expertise. I'd like to thank my brother, a retired Army Command Sergeant Major, who sat beside me as we transited the Panama Canal and discussed the best ways to temporarily close it down. Thank you both for your invaluable input!

CHAPTER 1

"Sir, the last passenger just disembarked. We have three carryover cabins," Andrew Buchanan's second-in-command announced over the security department radio.

"Roger." *Hot damn.* That meant that both he and Kendra were free for about thirty minutes before she had to take reports from the bridge staff and prepare to leave the terminal pier. The ship's master, Captain Phillips, would be doing the VIP Meet and Greet so Andrew knew she didn't need to change into her formal uniform.

He climbed the staff stairway three steps at a time. Glancing into the bridge, he was reassured that she was not there. Lieutenant Commander Adams strutted around, obviously in charge. Andrew keyed his way into the private corridor leading to the senior officers' quarters.

He smiled when the door to his cabin cracked

open one inch. Kendra was the only other person who had a key. They met in his room because as staff captain, her cabin was right next to Captain Phillips'. Fraternization rules were nowhere near as strict as they'd been in the Navy, but since technically she was his boss, neither wanted the accusations.

He glanced up and down the empty hallway before he casually opened his door and stepped in. Sweeping her into his arms, he immediately crashed his lips on hers.

"We have twenty-six minutes before I have to be back on the bridge." Kendra started unbuckling his belt as he grabbed his white uniform shirt by the back of the collar and pulled it over his head. He deftly slid it onto the hanger next to her uniform blouse. Since the cruise ship was rolling over passengers, both were required to be perfectly pressed all damn day.

Andrew toed off his shiny white shoes and slipped out of his socks, placing everything hurriedly next to hers. Both had been U.S. Navy officers before joining the cruise line so they knew how to get dressed, and undressed, in seconds.

Nearly naked, he cupped her face with his hands, sliding his fingers into her soft collar-length brown hair. "One day we're going to take our time and do this right."

"Sorry, Andrew, but today is not that day." She

lifted her face until her lips met his, wrapping her arms around his T-shirt–clad shoulders. "Besides, you do it quite right as far as I'm concerned."

Andrew gathered Kendra in his arms, running his hand down her spine while deepening the kiss. With a snap of his fingers, he unhooked her utilitarian white bra. He brought his hands forward, planning to move the straps down her arms.

Her cell phone chirped three loud beeps while vibrating.

His hands immediately stopped.

Kendra sighed and dropped her forehead to his T-shirt–covered chest. They both knew that indicated a very important message.

She reached over to his nightstand and grabbed her still buzzing phone. After scanning the message, she let out a long breath and collapsed on the side of his bed. "Captain Phillips suddenly has to go into Fort Lauderdale on ship's business and needs me to take over the VIP welcome."

One corner of Andrew's mouth kicked up sarcastically. "Surprise, surprise." He sat down beside her and threw his arm around her soft shoulders. "You do such a wonderful job of making nice with the important passengers." It was true. Captain Phillips could come across as very gruff, but the bridge staff had learned that was simply his personality. Andrew wrote it off as being German.

In his twelve years as a SEAL, he'd been through Germany several times and found the people to be cautious. They didn't seem to make friends quickly and it took a long time for them to trust. They also didn't waste words. Why say five, which included the word please, when one would do? He was also very large and imposing with a booming voice.

Kendra was the opposite. Although she expected her staff to do their job, she was also quick to compliment. As they had both been taught in the Navy, you praise in public and punish in private. Her feminine voice could definitely be commanding, but her easy smile and leadership techniques made her subordinates want to please her by doing their very best.

"I swear, since I made captain, he's given me all the jobs he hates the most. Last cruise I did five captain's tables while he hid out on the bridge." She turned in his arms to face him. "I'm perfectly capable of running the ship and he knows it. Hell, I commanded a U.S. Navy LPD in heavy seas as part of a carrier strike force."

He kissed the top of her head. "You know why he wants you on the receiving line; you are a beautiful woman with an outgoing personality that also wears captain's stripes. He wants the guests to feel welcome. I'm sure he's aware of his demeanor." Andrew chuckled. "When I first met him, his smile looked forced, and he seemed to search constantly for the right words in English. You don't have that problem at all."

"But this is our last cruise together." She tilted her head to face him. Normally she smiled back at him, but today sadness filled her beautiful golden eyes.

He hugged her tight to him. "Babe, we'll only be separated for three weeks." A shot of fear pierced his heart. "You are still planning on joining me in Miami after you finish your contract, aren't you?"

Her smile was reassuring before she leaned up and gave him a soft kiss. "Absolutely." She pecked his lips again and grinned. "And as soon as I get there, we're going to take our time, slowly stripping each other, kissing each revealed inch of naked skin." She placed kisses over his chin and down his throat. "We're going to slowly explore each other's body." She nipped at the hollow in his collarbone. "And sex will be completely unhurried and delicious." She pulled up his white cotton T-shirt and ran her fingertips over his defined abdomen muscles then pinched his flat nipples.

He grabbed her hand before she made him rock hard.

His watch buzzed. Glancing at the face, he read the text: *problem. bow linemen. ours.*

5

"Fuck." Andrew grabbed his shirt and slid it over his head. "I gotta go." Tucking it into his trousers, he gave himself a quick onceover. Pleased that his uniform maintained the creases even though he'd been up since four o'clock and all over the ship, he started to sniff his armpits then remembered he was heading to the bow lines. He'd have to change his shirt when he was finished so it didn't matter if it smelled like sweat at that moment. It was going to get a lot worse.

Leaning over the bed, he gave Kendra one long kiss. "You still have time to catch a combat nap."

She shook her head and stood. "I've got to shower and get into my dress uniform." Her smile was resolved.

"That should only take a few extra minutes," he noted as he picked up his crisp white hat.

"We're required to wear pantyhose, so it takes me considerably longer to get dressed than you. The cruise line is very sexist when it comes to appropriate attire for women. Females are required to wear dresses and skirts with heels." She picked up her durable everyday shoes. "You know I'd rather be in these and slacks."

"Yep. And I'd rather be in combat utilities but neither of us get our way." He grinned. "When you captain your own ship, you can change that."

She gave him an evil smile. "You're right. The master has those privileges."

Kendra stepped into her slacks and slid her feet into the shoes without lacing them. "Will you check the hall on your way out?" Buttoning her blouse, she added, "I'm hoping I can make it to my cabin without being seen."

"Sure." Andrew gave her one last short kiss and reached for the door. "Since you're doing VIP welcome, you'll get to greet my buddies before I do."

"I take it you got them VIP passes?" she asked while glancing at herself in the mirror, running her fingers through her hair where he had mussed it up.

"Yeah." Andrew knew he'd used his position as security officer to finagle a great price for the unfilled cabins, then bribed the hotel director for VIP passes for his former SEAL buddies, but what the hell. This was his last cruise, at least for a while.

His contract ended when they returned to Fort Lauderdale. After cruising for the last three months all over the Caribbean and through the Panama Canal, he deserved some fun in the sun. When he took the job as security officer, he liked the idea of being on a ship once again. Wearing commander's stripes on a white uniform that was so similar to the one he'd worn for twelve years in the Navy went a long way to boosting his personal morale. He would've been a commander by now if...

No. He wouldn't allow himself to go there.

He checked the hallway to assure it was empty then gave her one last kiss before heading to the bow.

"I'll take good care of your friends." She gave him a salacious grin. "You can take good care of me later in thanks."

* * *

KENDRA PASTED on her professional smile and dutifully greeted each of the VIP guests. She stood at the end of the receiving line as the highest-ranking officer present. Most guests had passed retirement years ago and had spent much of their newly discovered freedom aboard cruise ships.

"Welcome aboard." Kendra thought she recognized the couple in their seventies. "I'm Captain Benson."

"Harrison and Esther Harrington." The man held out his hand and she gave it her usual firm shake. She'd learned as she rose in rank in the U.S. Navy that eye contact and a firm handshake made an impression of strength.

"We have over three hundred nights aboard ships with Monarch Cruise Line alone," Esther announced. "Harrison and I have cruised several different lines. Personally, I prefer those where appropriate dress is required for supper." She sighed. "But the Panama Canal was on Harrison's bucket list, and this was the next ship heading there so he insisted we book a suite." This time she scowled. "Since all the larger ones were taken, we had to settle for a cabin in your new exclusive area."

Her gaze swept down the VIP line and abruptly stopped on four large, muscled men in desperate need of haircuts a month ago, wearing plaid shirts and jeans. They did look a bit out of place mixed in with septuagenarians, rising wannabes dressed to impress, and wealthy couples anxious to get away.

I'll bet those are Andrew's friends.

Esther sneered. "We'll see how exclusive your private area is."

Kendra bit back her comment about the military men who had fought for her freedom. Instead, she clenched her back teeth and bared two rows of straight pearly whites. "I'm sure you'll enjoy our butler service and private pool in our new Sanctuary, as well as the very large suites. I'm sure you'll enjoy our secluded dining room that offers exclusive meal choices. The Sanctuary also has an exclusive viewing deck where you want to be as we enter the canal."

The elderly woman seemed more pleased as Kendra guided her to the VIP host who would show the Harringtons to their cabin.

The next few couples were quick and cordial.

Next in line were the four casually dressed men. Kendra had spent enough time in the Navy to recognize a military man in civilian clothes. There was just something about them; their stance, keen awareness of their surroundings, something.

"Welcome aboard." She gave the first one a true smile and held out a hand in greeting.

"It's a pleasure to be aboard your ship, Captain Benson. Do cruise lines have many female captains?" He cringed. "I'm sorry, ma'am. That came out all wrong. I'm used to the Navy where we have very few female line officers."

She laughed boldly and let down her guard just a little. "Me too. I used to be one of those few female line officers. Now I'm the staff captain aboard this cruise ship." At the confused look on his face, she clarified, "It's the equivalent of the executive officer aboard a Navy vessel. You must be Andrew Buchanan's friends."

"Yes, ma'am, we are." The first man glanced over his shoulder at the other three.

"Andrew is our ship's security officer. He's busy right now but asked me to personally greet you."

"Ah." He smiled. "Well, thank you. That wasn't necessary. We didn't expect him to be able to be here waiting for us. I'm sure there are a million things on his plate before we get underway later this afternoon."

"Indeed." Kendra stared at the dark brown-haired man. She realized he wasn't going to offer his name. "I'd like to get to know all of you over the next eleven days since you are important enough to him to invite you on his last cruise. And you are…"

"Oh, yes, ma'am. I'm Grant Housman."

The next man stepped up and held out his hand. "Tavis Neade. It's a pleasure to meet you, ma'am."

"Keene Soto, but you can call me Gramps. Everyone does."

"Not sure I'll be able to call you that." Kendra shook her head. "I doubt you're much older than me and I certainly don't want to be called Grandma since I don't even have children."

"Ignore him." The last man shoved Keene out of the way and took both of Kendra's hands. "I'm Holden Billings and I look forward to spending as much time with you as you can spare."

As she deftly slid her hands from his, she noticed his right arm had several surgical scars. Kendra couldn't wait to get more information about each of Andrew's friends. She just hoped he didn't get angry with Holden. She actually found the man charming. Not her type, but attractive and delightful. She would bet his internal scars were far worse than those on his arms.

"Now you have a hint as to why his handle is Loki," Keene explained.

She didn't want to get into handles or nicknames, because she hated hers. It was just another reason to leave the Navy behind. She changed the subject; she leaned in and said quietly so none of the other passengers heard, "I believe Andrew is going to give you a tour of the ship. We don't do behind the scenes tours anymore, but Andrew thought you'd be interested."

"That would be cool," Holden stated. "We're overly familiar with a lot of ships, but none of them have been cruise ships." He chuckled as he adjusted the strap of his backpack on his shoulder.

"Well, you'll find that you don't have to duck your heads on this ship," Kendra joked. "Nor will you be bunking with dozens of people in stacked racks."

Grant laughed. "That's good to know. We'd also like to request as little drama as possible if you can arrange it," he teased. "We're not in the mood for pirates or enemy ships."

"Enemy ships are incredibly unlikely." She leaned in once again and whispered, "Pirates do happen from time to time, but not often while touring the Panama Canal. Mediterranean cruises and Suez Canal, that's a different story."

She stood straight, squared her shoulders, and

spoke so everyone in line could hear her. "Just a relaxing eleven-day cruise. Four ports including the canal. Sunshine. Evening entertainment. All the food you can eat." Lowering her voice for them, she added, "I promise the mess halls on this ship have much better food than a military ship."

Tavis nodded agreement. "Food. Perfect answer. I need a beer and a burger."

When her phone buzzed, Kendra excused herself and took a step back. She didn't hide the smile when she saw it was from Andrew. She quickly joined the four men. "Both of those can be arranged. As soon as you get to your cabin, call room service and place the order. You can enjoy the burger while you get settled and down that first beer. Andrew wants you to meet him back here in an hour for a tour. How does that sound?"

"Excellent," Grant agreed. "I'm really looking forward to that beer, but I do want to tour the ship and see Andrew."

Kendra handed them off to their VIP escort who happened to be a beautiful young woman on their hotel staff. She smiled as all four men flirted with her.

CHAPTER 2

THE ATRIUM WAS BUSTLING WITH NEW GUESTS exploring their home for the next eleven days when Andrew stepped to the end of the customer service counter. Knowing where his friends' cabins were located, he kept glancing in the direction he figured they would come. Automatically he scanned the crowd for any sign of trouble.

When his friends emerged, he didn't bother to be the stern security officer and hold back the grin that spread ear to ear. Until that moment, he hadn't realized how much he missed having true friends. Sure, he'd made solid acquaintances on the ship. He had several men who would gladly join him for a beer or a meal, but they all knew they'd only be together for few months and after that they'd probably never see each other again.

In all honesty, he didn't bother making the

lifetime friends that he had while in the U.S. Navy SEALs. That took years of depending on each other in life-or-death situations. Flying bullets changed the dynamic of any friendship and the likelihood of that happening on a cruise ship was nil.

Grant Housman, a friend since BUD/S, was the first to embrace him. "Damn, you look great."

"Thank you. I feel pretty damn good, too." Andrew realized it wasn't the normal platitude he'd give another officer on board the cruise ship. His stress level was nonexistent. After living on the edge most of his adult life, this job was a cakewalk. "I stay in shape, work out in the gym every day. I also run every morning." He didn't bother to tell them that he didn't jog alone. Most mornings lately he and Kendra ran side-by-side.

As an afterthought, he added, "I do miss swimming. It's not often that I get the day off while we're in port so I can swim in the ocean. Using the pools is frowned upon, even in the middle of the night." He discovered that no-no the first week on board. He'd been restless and headed to the nearest pool at three a.m. On about lap ten, a ball bounced off his head. When he'd stopped to yell at whomever had thrown it, he found Kendra standing at the end of the pool with her hands on her hips. Not exactly a great way to meet the other captain on board. These days, they laughed about the first time they met...

but he still wasn't allowed to swim even when she was on duty.

"Thanks for the great digs, sir." Keene Solo gave him some brotherly slaps on the back. "We didn't expect a balcony but thanks for that."

"There'll be none of that *sir* shit here. I'm no longer your commanding officer," he reminded all four of them. It would take a long time for Andrew to get over the fact that he'd sent Keene, Tavis, and Holden into Ethiopia along with the rest of their platoon. Andrew had been responsible for their squad being presumed dead for several months while they had actually been captured and tortured.

As a lieutenant commander in charge of a Middle East troop rotation, he'd been ordered to send a platoon into Ethiopia. They'd had bad intelligence. Fucking CIA.

When an entire squad of eight highly trained Navy SEALs gets blown up to the point where nothing is left to retrieve or bury, the Navy goes looking for a scapegoat. Since Andrew had given the final orders, he was court-martialed, stripped of his Trident, and thrown out of the Navy even though he was only following orders sent from above. It was easier to blame the last officer in the line than punish someone wearing eagles or stars.

When it was later discovered that the platoon had not been killed but captured, there was no way in hell they were ever going to reinstate

Andrew Buchanan, no matter how stellar his record had been. The cover-up went all the way to the vice president. They'd quietly retired him with an honorable discharge and full VA benefits, but a lieutenant commander's retired pay wasn't enough to live off. Besides, at thirty-six he was too young and too ambitious not to work.

Pulling him out of his terrible thoughts, Tavis shook Andrew's hand and gave him a half hug. "Honestly, we would've been happy with interior rooms."

Holden stepped up, extending his hand. "But now that we're unpacked, we're not moving." Andrew was careful with his shake and embrace. He knew that the fucking Ethiopian rebels had broken his friend's arm time and time again to keep him in pain. The rod in Holden's arm that held the pieces together was still healing.

"Since this is my last cruise, at least for a few months, I was able to grab those two cabins side-by-side at the last minute." Andrew smiled at his four friends. "I'm so glad you guys were able to take advantage of my offer." He'd called the rest of their squad but none of the others were available. He'd do something else special for them.

Guilt had racked him for months over their torture. As the captain had brought out during his court-martial, if there was no DNA to be found, that could have meant they were still alive. Andrew should have gone looking for them. But

17

again, all CIA reports had indicated the rebels had killed them all in the explosion. Fucking CIA.

Andrew gestured toward the bow of the ship. "Let's start with the bridge and work our way down."

"So, s—," Tavis stopped mid word. "Exactly what is it that you want us to call you?"

"Andrew works." He grinned over his shoulder at the men who were all around his age. "That is my name. Unless you want to be eating my fist, don't *ever* call me Andy." Now that there weren't the officer/enlisted fraternization rules, they could be friends.

"How about we call you Zed? That was your handle in the SEALs," Tavis suggested.

Andrew shook his head and for a moment he couldn't say anything. Those days were bitter-sweet memories and seemed so far away.

He'd loved being a SEAL officer, commanding the best men in the world, but when they'd stripped his Trident, they'd taken part of his soul. A computer change in his military status and the monthly check in the bank couldn't repair the hole in his heart.

He swallowed the lump in his throat. "Those days are over. I'm now Commander Buchanan, security officer aboard this cruise ship." He opened the Staff Only door and started climbing the stairs. The other men fell in single file up the narrow stairwell. Many of the lessons he'd learned on Navy ships applied to this vessel, including stairway etiquette.

Four flights of industrial stairs later when they'd all stepped out into the carpeted hallway, Andrew began with a few facts. "This is a medium-size cruise ship. Guest capacity is three thousand eighty, but we only have two thousand two hundred fifty-two on board right now. Of the fifteen hundred forty-one guest cabins, over three hundred are vacant." Smiling at his friends, he added, "That's why I was able to get you such a damn good deal."

"S…Andrew, we can't thank you e—" Holden started but Andrew held up his hand like a traffic cop.

"Enough, already." He gave them a genuine smile. "It was truly my pleasure." He continued, "We're at full capacity for crew, which is twelve hundred. Almost all of them live on the lower decks in tiny cabins shared with one or two people depending on their position. They live much closer to the way we lived on Navy ships. They have their own dining hall down there, too. Sorry, but I'm forbidden to show you that area." He tapped the gold stripes on his shoulder boards. "Besides, if I show up down there, they'll think somebody's in big trouble."

Andrew continued in his formal tour guide voice, "When the crew is not at work, they're not to be seen in the public areas. Most of them put in twelve- to sixteen-hour days. Their contracts are usually six months or more."

At Andrew's signal they followed him to the locked glass door at the end of the hall that looked onto the sparse bridge. "When the ship was refurbished in 2019, it upgraded the navigation." He chuckled. "This bridge doesn't look anything like that of an aircraft carrier even though we can carry almost the same number of people."

Each man stepped up to the glass and peered through.

"It doesn't look like there's enough switches and dials to drive the ship." Keene was correct.

"The first time I walked onto the bridge I was shocked," Andrew continued to explain, "Like you, I was looking for the huge gray boxes covered with toggle switches and a wheel in the middle." The Hollywood over-exaggerated pirate ship wheel hadn't been around for a century, but most Navy ships could be controlled by a semi-truck-sized steering wheel if needed.

"The ship doesn't even have a rudder so a wheel would be useless." Andrew pointed out the side window to the long extension of the bridge. "This ship has nearly a dozen pods that can be turned three hundred sixty degrees. It works beautifully for docking. Those controls are way out there at the end on each side."

"Where are the chart tables?" Tavis asked.

"This ship is paperless. No old-fashioned charts to lay out," Andrew explained. "Everything is computerized. The ship can be placed on autopilot and do almost everything except dock. The computer auto corrects for current and wind."

He then added, "We often pick up a local pilot who is familiar with the complexities of that specific water. If you watch carefully while we're in Limón Bay, just before we enter the waterway to the Panama locks, you'll see us pick up a local pilot who will stay with us until we go back through the locks."

"As the security officer, do you have to vet each one of those men?" Holden had asked a good question.

Andrew shook his head. "No. The cruise line is responsible for that. My men meet him at the waterline, check his ID then escort him to the bridge. One of my men stays with him the entire time."

"Are you telling me that you don't even search him for weapons?" The incredulity on Keene's face matched that of Grant, Tavis, and Holden.

"No, that's one of the things that I hate about this job." Andrew whispered even though no one was in the hallway. "Sometimes, the pilot comes on board with his own guards. I'm talking armed military men. Kendra gets creeped out when she has the ship's controls, and they show up."

"Kendra, huh." Leave it to Holden to catch that little slip. "So, you and the pretty little captain got it going on?"

What the hell. He mentally shrugged. These were his friends, and this was his last cruise... maybe. "Yeah. She and I have been together for the last month." Or was it longer? He certainly didn't want to have this conversation in the middle of the hallway where any of the bridge crew could overhear. "Let me show you my quarters and you'll realize how good you have it." As he stepped toward the locked hall, he realized he'd just used the naval term instead of cabin. In only minutes he'd already fallen into military jargon.

After unlocking and entering the restricted area, he met the gaze of several bridge crew who stood talking in the hallway. Most nodded and they all returned to their previous conversation.

In his best tour guide voice, Andrew explained, "Normally this area is off limits to everyone except those of us who live here, but since you're my brothers I wanted to show you where I live."

As soon as he opened his door, Tavis loudly declared, "It's a damn sight better than anywhere you slept while in the Navy."

"How are you able to sleep in here when it's not battleship gray?" Holden joked.

The men followed him into the room that

suddenly felt very small. When he was alone, or with Kendra, he thought of his cabin as normal. With five former SEALs crammed in, claustrophobia niggled at his nerves.

"Well, this is it." Andrew forced a smile as he tried to see his room through their eyes. It was rather barren of anything personal. On his desk he had a picture of his family taken at his sister's wedding last summer with her in her gown. He and all his brothers were clean-shaven and in tuxedos as well as his father. His mother was in a pretty light blue dress, her smile so proud of her family.

"Not bad for a ship but thanks again for getting us those awesome cabins with a balcony." Grant patted him twice on the shoulder and turned toward the door.

Holden held it closed. "Not so fast. Now that we're alone, what's the deal with you and the cute captain?"

Andrew wasn't sure how much to tell them. "She's former Navy, an Academy grad like me. We didn't know each other back then. She was a few years ahead of me."

"Oooh. An older woman," Holden teased.

"Found yourself a cougar, huh?" Tavis made a cat sound and clawed his fingers through the air.

"Shut the fuck up, you babies," Keene, whose handle was Gramps, chastised the others. "Good for you for finding some action while aboard a ship...unless the cruise line has fraternization rules too."

"No, but it's certainly not encouraged." He shrugged. "She's only three years older than me and at our age, that doesn't mean shit. Besides, this is my last cruise on this contract."

"Are you then headed to Indiana?" Grant asked.

Indiana? Andrew was a little confused.

"Didn't you take the deal with the Holt Agency?" Tavis raised his eyebrows.

"Oh, yeah. It seems like forever ago when Ryker and Ajax called me." Andrew huffed. "I wasn't exactly in a good place when I talked to them." He'd just been stripped of his Trident, publicly kicked out of the Navy, and had no prospects for a job. The offer to work for the Holt Agency sounded good.

Then he'd gotten a call from Charley. Her offer sounded even better. By the end of that week, he'd boarded this cruise ship with a sweet, easy job that included a place to stay. It seemed as though his angel had solved all of his problems. So much had happened for him personally in the past three months that he hadn't thought about the Holt Agency since.

"So, are you going to join us in Indiana after you finish this cruise?" Keene sounded hopeful.

"I'll be honest, I really don't know." Andrew needed to consider the Holt Agency offer a little bit more before he signed his next Monarch Cruise Line contract. "I've made enough money from this cruise gig to take off a month or two. I have a place in Miami that I'll go to and just veg, maybe dive a little, and swim in a warm ocean every day."

"I don't know what it's like to swim in a warm ocean." Tavis shook his head and chuckled. "When I heard I was going to BUD/S, I thought the water in San Diego would be warm."

All five men laughed out loud.

"I'll bet you were disappointed on our first mile ocean swim." Holden shoulder-punched Tavis.

"I prayed I'd get an East Coast assignment after BUD/S. I knew the water would be warmer in Virginia Beach," Grant admitted.

"I'm so glad we all got stationed in the East Coast." At Keene's declaration, all the men nodded in agreement.

"Let's go see the rest of the boat." Grant opened the door and headed back to the stairs.

"We'll take the crew elevator down." Andrew pointed to doors hidden in a wall. "Is anybody interested in seeing the engines?"

"Sure, why the hell not," Keene said as he stepped in last.

"I'm excited about some of these ports. The Bahamas sound wonderful. I'll bet they have warm water." Tavis grinned. "I could use a day at the beach watching nubile young women in teeny tiny bikinis."

"How you going to hide your hard-on in a pair of board shorts?" Holden nudged him.

"Can't tell I'm hard in the water." Tavis's grin widened.

Andrew chuckled. "You might be able to in that water. It's so clear you can see the bottom at thirty-five feet."

This time Tavis laughed. "Then it's a damn good thing I don't wear a Speedo. I'd be peeking out of the top."

"To quickly change the subject because I don't have any brain bleach to erase the gross picture my mind just painted, I'm thinking about signing up for an excursion. What are they like, Andrew?" Grant looked his way.

"I couldn't really tell you because as ship security officer I'm really busy while in port." Smiling, he continued, "I'll get one day off this cruise and I'm definitely going to take advantage of it." He'd have to check with Kendra to see if she had the same day off. That would be a miracle. They could be just Andrew and Kendra off the ship.

"Are you on call all the time?" Keene asked as the doors opened.

"Yes. I have a really great second-in-command who can take over for several hours but if shit goes bad, I have to be there."

Donning sound suppressors, they stepped out onto the catwalk above the huge engines.

Two hours later they stood in the atrium where they'd started. Andrew had shown them everything he could on the ship. "So, what did you think?"

"Pretty cool."

"In some ways it wasn't that different from an aircraft carrier...without planes and helicopters."

"And with much nicer quarters."

"I think I need a beer," Holden suggested. "Then a list of the best places to meet women."

"I'm sorry I can't hang out with you tonight. I'm on duty." Andrew rattled off the names of several nightclubs and bars, making note of the more popular ones.

CHAPTER 3

KENDRA HAD JUST FINISHED CLIPPING HER HEART monitor around her ribs and tucking the belt under her compression bra when her phone buzzed with the text: *on 19 stretching*

Her reply was brief: *OMW*. She always abbreviated *on my way*. Typing out the words took too long.

As she grabbed her keys on the way out the door, the feminine part inside her shook with excitement. She was heading to see Andrew. They'd missed each other most of the previous day, except for those few heated kisses before they were rudely interrupted by their jobs. Embarkation day was always busy for her as staff captain. Although her team all knew their jobs and handled them well, there always seemed to be something that required her attention, especially since Captain Phillips had been ashore.

She jogged up the stairs to the nineteenth deck. Her blood already pumping, she started to jog the designated red path. As she passed Andrew, she smacked him on the butt.

"Catch up, Commander." She checked her watch for her pulse rate. Eighty-six. That was an excellent start. As Andrew caught up to her, she increased her stride. At five foot nine she could never match his six one gait, but she loved the fact that with him by her side, she pushed herself. Kendra knew he shortened his steps to match hers as they quickly circled the deck.

At the end of her first lap, she checked her smart watch. Ninety-nine. Pleased with her pace, she had plenty of breath to talk. "I take it wasn't anything serious with the lineman yesterday."

"Hell, no." Andrew was still breathing steadily through his nose. "I think my security officer just wanted to flex some muscle in front of the local dockworker. He's new. He should have called his sergeant, not me. All my men know calling me is a last resort."

Kendra chuckled. "I'll bet he never does it again."

Andrew glanced to the side and gave her a quick smile. "I can guarantee it. I brought all my sergeants together as soon as we left the pier and we set up training to make sure the new man learns how we do things on this ship and to remind those who've been here a while."

"That sounds like an excellent idea." She thought about her own staff and how many new crewmembers had come aboard in the past month. Hotel staff rotated on nine-month contracts; food and beverage varied but many were on six-month rotations, especially bartenders. They were almost always the ones to break the rules, particularly about personal fraternization with guests. They got laid more often than anyone else. Since the ship had been back in operation for nearly a year after being dormant for eighteen months during COVID, everybody could use a refresher.

"What are you going to do after the staff meeting this morning? Are you still on twelve to twelve today?"

Grinning, she glanced over her shoulder. "Got something personal in mind?"

"When it comes to you, doll, I've always got something personal in mind."

She still cringed at the term of endearment. When he'd first called her that she wasn't happy. One afternoon, naked in bed, he called her doll and she pinned him on it.

"Well, when we first started…seeing each other, Kendra sounded so formal. There was no way in hell I could bring myself to shorten your name to Ken. I almost needed brain bleach to erase that plastic, dickless doll from my mind. But the word doll just kinda stuck in my head."

Then he'd kissed her and ran his hands from the crown of her head to her hips. "You're like a perfectly proportioned, life-size doll. Tall and slender." He bent down and nipped her nipple then grinned up at her. "But unlike those fake little toys, you have all the anatomically correct parts." He then proceeded to point out every anatomical difference with his tongue and mouth. The way he'd made her come, he could call her anything he wanted to.

"Kendra, you okay?" His question jolted her out of the wonderful memory.

"Yeah." Her smile was salacious as she glanced up at him. "I was actually thinking about how much I miss you. We haven't been able to see each other in days."

"Not true. We see each other every day."

She knew he was teasing. Two could play that game, and she played dirty. "I don't get to see the parts of you I want to kiss..." She took two steps and leaned closer to whisper. "And lick." Two more steps. "And suck."

"Enough." He stopped running and shoved her into a shadow, hiding them both behind a steel beam. "How the hell do you expect me to run with a hard-on? I'm sorry about yesterday morning. Believe me, I was in more pain than you were. I want you so much." He bent his head and kissed her.

She thought it would be hard, fast, and needy. Instead, it was sweet and tender.

Kendra melted into him. She loved the feeling of his strong arms around her. She immediately opened for him, his tongue diving in and capturing hers.

They must've heard the voices at the same time because they broke apart. Her heart was pounding so fast she checked her watch. One hundred eighteen.

Andrew glanced down the track then toward the sun that had just peeked over the horizon. "The guests are starting to move around so let's sprint back to the staff door."

"You're on." Kendra took off at a full run. They had to make it all the way to the other end of the ship. Andrew passed her easily but waited for her at their door before walking beside her down the stairs.

They didn't speak until they got to the officer hallway. Thankfully it was empty when she pulled him into her room. The smell of coffee was heavenly. Each poured a cup and took it with them to the balcony. They sat in her comfortable lounge chairs, sipping coffee and taking deep breaths to bring down their heart rates.

"You never did answer my question; what are you doing after the staff meeting?"

She knew what she wanted to do: drag his ass back to her bed, have at least two orgasms, then fall asleep and take a nap. "I'm not sure. What did you have in mind?"

"I'm on duty twelve to twelve, same as you, right?" His beautiful hazel eyes held hers.

"Yes."

He reached over and took her hand. "Then I want you in my bed. Bring your uniform." He lightly squeezed her fingers. "This is my last cruise and I want to spend every moment I can with you. I want to fall asleep next to you whenever we can." He set his coffee mug on the small table between them and sat up, facing her, never letting go of her hand. "Kendra, our time together has been awesome, and I don't want it to stop when I leave this ship."

Was he saying what she thought he was saying? Did he want to continue the relationship after the ship returned to the USA?

"I've rented a place in Miami. On the beach. It isn't much, just your typical beach rental." He squeezed her hand. "I know you have another month on your contract on the ship, but would you consider spending some time with me in between cruises?" Before she could answer he continued, "And after your contract is up?"

Oh, my gosh. He really wants to spend more time with me. I haven't felt this way about a man in years. Not since I first started dating my asshole ex. Shit. I haven't told Andrew about him. It doesn't matter. Andrew is the only thing that matters.

"Yes." Leaping off her chair, she threw her arms around him, straddling his lap. She kissed him with all the emotion she felt inside, trying to tell him with her mouth and tongue what her words wouldn't say. She wanted to spend more time with him. Uninterrupted. She wanted to get to know him even better. She wanted him for longer than a few stolen hours. She wanted him.

She regretted how she'd ignored him the first month he was on board, keeping every interaction extremely professional. Not just with Andrew, but with everyone.

She'd only been on that ship a few weeks under the former captain who was quite friendly, as in too friendly. It had gotten even worse when Monarch Cruise Line announced that she had been promoted to captain. Even though he only had a few weeks left as master of that ship, he'd pursued her constantly. Relentlessly. She was so happy the day he walked down the gangway for the last time.

When Captain Phillips took over the ship, it took everyone a few cruises to become accustomed to his command style. During his first cruise, he ordered his senior officers to dine with him. He wanted to know everyone's background, not just what was in their personnel file.

Kendra had been shocked to hear that Andrew attended the Naval Academy and had been a U.S. Navy SEAL commanding officer.

The bridge was filled with men from all over the world. It felt wonderful to know another American was there with her. That was the exact moment she'd started to see Andrew differently.

Sitting on his lap, staring into his hazel eyes that now looked closer to the blue in his T-shirt, she regretted all the time she'd wasted trying to keep him at arm's length. "I'm sorry I was such a bitch to you when you first came on board."

He cocked his head to the side. "Are you talking about the incident in the pool? That wasn't your fault. It was mine. Look, I'm really sorry, but I swear I never read that in the rules."

She leaned forward and laid a light kiss on his lips. "No, I'm not talking about that. I was harsh back then, to everybody, but especially to you." She pecked his lips once again. "I didn't want anyone to think that I was available. The previous captain...he..."

Andrew sat up straighter and grabbed her shoulders. "Did he touch you?"

"Hell, no. He tried as soon as I came on board. And failed." She didn't want to waste their time together talking about him. "He's gone and hopefully I'll never have to see him again because I will be the master of my own ship after this."

Leaning in, she kissed him, only breaking apart to hug him. Her lips next to his ear, she whispered, "Let's take this to my bed."

After glancing at his watch, he slid his hands under her butt and picked her up.

She immediately wrapped her long legs around his waist, enjoying the way he took control. As soon as he set her down, she stripped out of her stinky clothes, tossing them in the hamper.

"No complaints here," he said as he shucked his running shorts and dark blue shirt to the side.

She sat on the bed as they both kicked off their shoes and slid off their socks. Naked, he stood in front of her, his cock standing proud. Damn, this man always seemed ready.

Kendra licked the tip of his jutting cock then pulled him down onto the mattress. "You on bottom. I want to ride you." Mostly because she knew their time was limited and he was so good with his hands and mouth.

His only reply was to pull her on top of him, deftly separating her folds with his fingers, testing her already wet center. "You've been thinking about this."

"I told you I missed you." She straddled his hips and guided him inside her.

They'd had *the talk* after the fourth time they'd had sex. She'd known at that point she wanted more with him, and only him. They were both certified clean and disease free before starting their contracts—and neither had been with anyone since boarding the ship—so they decided to do away with condoms since she was on the pill.

"Fuck, there's no better feeling than you bareback." Andrew leaned up and took one of her breasts in his mouth, sucking hard the way she liked it. She didn't know how it was possible, but it seemed her breasts and clit were somehow attached. He had discovered that connection that no other man had found.

She raised her hips then slammed down on him as he arched up into her. Both his hands cupped her breasts, kneading them, rolling and pinching her nipples as they met and separated. They'd become quite good at this.

Andrew seemed to realize that her orgasm was elusive that morning. He dropped one hand from her breast to her mound, his thumb finding her clit. He pressed, circled, then found the bottom of her bundle of nerves and pushed up.

Kendra flew over the edge, taking Andrew with her. She collapsed on his bare chest, her head dropping to the crook of his neck. His powerful arms wrapped around her, making her feel protected. She caught a whiff of his scent and that's all it took to put her to sleep.

CHAPTER 4

"THANK YOU FOR GREETING MY FRIENDS yesterday." Andrew slid into his white slacks, glad Kendra had suggested he keep a complete work uniform in her cabin for just such occasions. They hadn't overslept but at her suggestion of showering together, he wasn't going to say no. Round two in the shower did put them a few minutes behind.

"You're welcome." She rolled her eyes. "Lieutenant Commander Adams told me that you brought your 'brothers' to your cabin yesterday."

"Fucking tattletale." He slid his already buttoned shirt over his head. He could get dressed faster than any man she knew. "That would have been a breach of security and he should have brought it to me. But, oh, gosh almighty, I'm the one who brought them to my secure quarters."

Kendra glanced over at him, adjusting her breasts in her basic white bra. "Quarters? Don't you mean cabin?"

"Fuck, yes. I did that yesterday around my men, too." He sat on the unmade bed and slid on his socks before grabbing his shiny white shoes. "I'm surprised the little snitch hasn't complained to Captain Phillips about our morning jog together."

Kendra laughed. "That would mean he'd have to get his growing ass out of bed before dawn. I don't think the man has seen this jogging track since he came on board, and I know damn well he hasn't been in the gym. But he certainly hasn't missed any meals. Every time I turn around, he's got a cup of soft ice cream in his hand."

"I guess he's a *do as I say and not as I do* leader. He was ragging on Ensign Dudley last week for her sucker when I escorted one of the local pilots to the bridge. I can't stand the pompous ass. You'd think he was an expert on handling the bridge."

"He has the ship skills but certainly not the people skills." Kendra stood.

"One of these days he's gonna run his mouth to the wrong person." Andrew hoped it was him on his last day aboard the ship. "I knew a few like him back in the Navy. They never would have made it to lieutenant."

"He came to us from the Italian Merchant

Marine Academy. That's supposed to be a pretty good school even though it's relatively new. According to his vetting file, he applied to all of the American and Australian military academies including the U.S. Merchant Marine Academy. He didn't have the grades to get in any of those and he wasn't able to pass the basic physical fitness test."

Andrew raised his eyebrows. "You can look at that shit?" Concern shot straight to his gut. Had Kendra looked at his vetting file? Did she know he'd been court-martialed? He'd purposely been extremely vague with her as to why he'd gotten out of the military. Up until the point he'd sent that platoon into Ethiopia, he had an impressive career, especially if she had the security clearance to read about all of his missions. He'd been a damn good SEAL.

"Yes, I have access to it, but I don't look at it unless I have a reason. I wanted to find out if Lieutenant Commander Adams had taken any of the Monarch Cruise Line classes, especially the ones on leadership. As staff captain it's my responsibility to identify possible problem areas and to develop junior officers' leadership skills."

"I thought he was Greek." Andrew wasn't sure why he'd thought that, maybe he'd overheard conversation talking about that part of the Mediterranean.

"No. He's actually a South African citizen but

his parents were from Italy. His father is a captain driving oil tankers coming out of the Middle East and running down to the tip of Africa. I guess his father used to take him along during summers. He brags about outrunning pirates in the Gulf of Aden."

"Not like he'll have to do anything like that here." Andrew grabbed his hat.

Kendra turned her face up to his and kissed him. "I'll see you at the morning briefing." She stepped into the hall and immediately spoke to other people, letting him know he needed to stay put for a few minutes.

Forty minutes later, Andrew was the last one to leave the briefing. "Not bad for the first day."

"Other than a few cabin mix-ups, and Commander Jessup is great at handling those, we had a pretty good day one." Kendra picked up her logbook and headed toward the bridge.

"Give them a few days of heat and alcohol and tempers will flare." Andrew grinned. "Who knows, maybe I'll get to use that brig before I leave."

"Just as long as we don't have to use the mobile morgue, I'm happy."

"Bite your tongue and perish the thought." There were a ton of paperwork when someone died on a cruise ship, no matter the cause. Andrew hated all the paperwork the cruise line required. Seemed like he spent most of his time at a computer.

Kendra looked up at him and smiled. Whispering close to his ear, she said, "I'd rather you bite my tongue…or somewhere else."

He looked around and no one was there so he bent and gave her a quick kiss. "I don't go on duty until noon today. Text me as you're heading back to your cabin. I'll help you sleep."

Her smile was inviting. "Perfect idea. You'll meet me there?"

"Provided there's no emergency." Andrew prayed there wouldn't be. He needed the nap and her.

* * *

THANK goodness he and Kendra had snoozed before they both went on duty. Around two-thirty in the afternoon he'd gotten a call that he was needed at the pool.

His two shortest sergeants, tough little Spanish guys, and three of his officers had separated the two men who were big enough to play linebacker for any pro football team. Although standing ten feet apart, they were still shouting at each other over the heads of his men.

"No fucking way they could win." The lighter-haired man stretched out his arm and pointed toward the other.

"You don't know what the fuck you're talking about," the man with dark curly hair screamed back.

His men were trying to do their job. "Sir, there are children around. Please refrain from using foul language."

Andrew approached the men and looked them eye to eye. "Gentlemen, I'm Commander Buchanan, security officer. I'm going to have to ask you to leave this area."

"I don't have to fucking leave if I don't want to." The lighter-haired man turned toward him, fists on his bare hips. Andrew glanced down just to be sure he was wearing a bathing suit because his large belly hid most of it.

The other man darted to stand right beside him, copying his pose. "We paid a hell of a lot of money to come on this cruise and we can be at this pool if we want to."

Glancing around, Andrew observed that they were the center of everyone's attention. "Gentlemen, how about we step over here in the shade off to the side to continue this conversation in private." He gestured to everyone whose eyes were on them.

"I don't give a flying fuck if they listen to us," the first one yelled over his shoulder. "Get out your fucking phones and video this. I'm going to need proof when I sue the hell out of this cruise line."

When he turned back, the smell of alcohol almost knocked Andrew over. "Gentlemen, did you by chance get the alcohol package as part of your cruise purchase?"

"Fuck, yes," they practically said in unison before they turned toward each other and high-fived.

"I take it you've been sitting out here in the sun drinking for several hours." Andrew's men had moved behind him as they'd been taught, showing a wall of force.

"Yeah, what of it?" the dark-haired man snapped.

"And that's another thing, that fucking bartender over there told me I couldn't have any more whiskey. You look like you outrank him, go tell him to give me another drink," the light-haired man demanded.

Andrew glanced toward the bar to find the food and beverage lieutenant commander standing next to his bartender giving Andrew the cutoff signal.

"Gentlemen, what do you think would happen if I gave you a breathalyzer test?" Andrew tried to remember where the device and the mouthpieces were. He never had to use one in the three months he worked as the security officer.

The men laughed drunkenly in his face. "Nothin'," the light-haired man said, breathing in his face. "We ain't driving."

"Did you read your entire contract when you purchased your cruise tickets?" Andrew asked, never raising his voice. "There are several paragraphs that refer to conduct aboard this vessel. Drunk and disorderly violates the terms of that agreement." He looked at his sergeant and barely gave a nod before stepping away and speaking quietly into his shoulder radio. "And according to that agreement, the captain has every right to remove you from this ship if you cause a disturbance."

"And if Commander Buchanan suggests that I do just that, I will." Kendra stepped up beside him. "Gentlemen, I believe you've had more than enough to drink. Now, I'll give you two choices. Number one, turn around and apologize to my guests for your rude behavior and foul language, then walk quietly to your cabins."

Andrew was so proud of her because her strong gaze never left the two much taller men.

"Your number two choice will be both painful and humiliating because most likely you will pee your pants." She looked over at Andrew and nodded once.

He gave the signal to his men to draw their weapons. Because it was illegal for commercial ships to carry guns that shot bullets, all his men pulled tasers that shot electrodes. From a distance, they looked like mean guns with very large barrels.

"I can tell you from experience that just one set of electrodes knocked me on my ass. I'll also share with you that there are sharp little barbs that are normally meant to attach to clothing." He let his gaze slowly drop over the men's nearly naked bodies. Shaking his head, he hissed, "That's gonna hurt."

He then turned and counted out loud before returning his gaze to the two large men in front of him. "At this range, my men won't miss. Each one of those tasers will give you fifty thousand volts of electricity." He cocked his head to the side. "You both look like you have a good strong heart, so you'll live through it." He looked from one man to the other. Then he grimaced. "If by chance one of those probes attaches to…sensitive parts of your body…" Andrew purposefully looked down at their very small bathing suits, "it might be a long time before those parts work."

Andrew had to school his face as both men placed their hands over their junk. But he didn't stop talking. "After we tase both of you, you'll be taken down to our jail, but here on the ship, we call that the brig. Looks like a jail, though, steel bars and all. Then it's up to the captain to decide what happens to you."

Kendra jumped in. "Our next port of call is Costa Rica day after tomorrow. You'll live in the brig until then. Shortly after we dock, you will be escorted off the ship. At that point, Monarch

Cruise Line has no responsibility for you. You have to find your own way home. I hope you speak fluent Spanish."

She clasped her hands in front of her. "So, gentlemen, what will it be, choice number one or choice number two?"

Andrew got worried when the two men said nothing, just looked at each other. A glance over his shoulder assured him that his men also prepared for attack.

"One!" both men said together.

Kendra nodded and waved her hand to the crowd mesmerized by the show.

Both men looked at their feet and slowly shuffled around to face their audience.

"Sorry." The word was mumbled toward the deck.

Kendra walked around to face them and squared her shoulders. "I'm sorry, did you say something?"

The word was repeated slightly louder.

"That's not the way my mama taught me to apologize. You look at the person, or in this case people, and tell them what you're sorry for."

There was a long pause before the light-haired man lifted his head. "I'm sorry." He glanced at Kendra then back at the audience. "For yelling at my brother here and swearing." He then looked to Kendra for approval.

Giving none, her eyes moved to the other man.

"I'm sorry for acting like an ass, I mean jerk." He too stopped his gaze on Kendra.

"Commander Buchanan, you have your men please escort these two gentlemen to their cabins."

"Yes, ma'am." And his men stepped up, one on each side, a sergeant behind each man.

Before they took a single step, Kendra spoke. "Gentlemen, I strongly suggest that you sleep off the overabundance of alcohol you've consumed today. I promise you that if you misbehave again on this cruise, I will personally escort you off at the next port of call and hand you over to the local police. Do you understand me?"

Both men nodded.

"I need a verbal confirmation."

"Yes, Captain."

"Yes, ma'am."

"Commander Buchanan, notify me immediately if you have any more problems with these two gentlemen. Take them to their cabins."

"Aye aye, ma'am." The minute the words came out of his mouth, Andrew cringed. Another Navy term not used on cruise ships.

Kendra threw him a look then fought a grin. He'd hear about that later, for sure.

Between Andrew's men and the security cameras, they kept track of the two recalcitrant men the rest of the day. When he saw them together heading toward the theater, he had three of his men meet him there. He stationed one of the sergeants from the earlier incident at each entrance. Sending the tallest officer he had to one side, he took the other set of double doors.

They'd only been waiting a few minutes when his friends and their dates arrived.

"Is everything okay?" Grant asked as he pulled a pretty blonde woman to the side next to him.

Andrew tilted his head and said just above a whisper, "We had some problems at the pool a few hours ago. It took Kendra coming down from the bridge and threatening to throw them off the ship at the next port if they didn't return to their cabins and sleep it off. My men followed them, but video showed them leaving their cabins and going to supper. Fortunately, they weren't seated near each other. We don't want any trouble here."

"Anything we can do?" Holden asked.

"Nah. Shit like this happens almost every cruise but not usually until about day five." Andrew shrugged. "I guess it's just going to be one of *those* cruises. Figures. My last cruise and there's already trouble on day two."

"You'll let us know if there's anything we can do to help?" Grant ran his hand up and down his date's spine. That was a lot of PDA for only the second day. Andrew wondered if his friend had already gotten lucky. He certainly hoped so. These four men deserved all the good news the world could give them.

Andrew smiled at his two friends and their lady guests. "Go enjoy the show. This guy's pretty good. Bones and Gramps are in there waiting for you." He then corrected himself. "Tavis and Keene saved you seats."

As they started to step away, Kendra approached with a huge smile. "I'm glad to see you're going to watch the magician." She leaned in and whispered, "This is one of my favorite shows." Glancing toward the women, she held out her hand. "I'm Captain Kendra Benson."

Grant's friend held out her hand. "Cal—"

"There they are." Andrew stepped forward toward two couples, Kendra on his heels.

"Gentlemen, a word, please." Andrew stretched out his arms and without touching anyone, herded the two couples off to the side out of the way of guests entering the theater. This time he would completely control the situation, starting in a semiprivate alcove.

Both women seemed wary. Obviously the men hadn't told their wives of their actions earlier that afternoon. *This ought to be fun.*

"Gentlemen, I trust that you have slept off some of the effects of your overabundance of alcohol consumption? Your appearance here together with indicate that you have solved your previous differences." Andrew's gaze bounced between the two men who kept glancing nervously toward the women at their sides.

"What the hell did you do?" The well-dressed brunette stepped back and looked up at the man with dark curly hair. When he didn't answer immediately, she looked directly into Andrew's eyes.

"There was an altercation at the pool between these two." Andrew decided perhaps the less said the better.

Kendra had no compunction to pull punches. "The volume and language they used was completely inappropriate to the point that I was called down from the bridge and threatened to remove them from the ship after Commander Buchanan threw them in the brig." At the women's confused faces, she clarified, "The jail on board the ship."

"Sir, I can promise you this one won't give you any more problems," the brunette in the fancy dress vowed.

"Or this big idiot." The blonde turned her attention toward her large husband. "Leave it to you to fuck up our one-year anniversary cruise."

"I'll bet this was over some damn football game." Dark hair flew as the first woman looked from one man then to the other.

"Hockey," the contrite men muttered in unison.

"Captain, I'm sorry, you'd think brothers would know how to get along together after thirty years." The blonde grabbed her husband's hand. "Come on. We'll go to the bar and talk about this."

"I think they've had more than enough to drink for today. Perhaps this should be a private conversation," Kendra suggested. She probably didn't want to get called down to another scene.

"She's right." The blonde followed suit. "What I have to say to you isn't fit for polite company." She grabbed her husband's hand and dragged him down the hall.

The men followed along, the blonde's husband mouthing *makeup sex* with a huge smile. His brother nodded, mirroring his smile.

"Well, if we have problems with them again, I guess we'll just find their wives." Andrew obviously fought a smile.

"I hope I'm not master of their ship when they celebrate their second anniversary." Kendra shook her head.

"I doubt they'll make it that long." Grant grinned.

"I'd take that bet." Holden held out his hand. "Their wives are going to end the night very satisfied...and so are they."

The lights in the theater blinked.

"You'd better go grab your seats, the show's

about to start." Andrew looked down at Kendra. "Are you staying for the show?"

"Yeah. It's one of my favorites. I'll watch from back here."

"Let's go grab a piece of wall." Andrew and Kendra followed his friends into the darkening theater.

CHAPTER 5

Kendra loved magic acts. She knew and understood they were all sleight-of-hand and illusion, but this guy was really good. She'd seen him several times over the years as she climbed the ladder of the Monarch Cruise Line.

After leaving the Navy, and her husband, she knew she wanted to captain her own ship one day. It had been a lifelong dream. Growing up in the Seattle area, practically surrounded by water, she'd taken her first water safety course at twelve so she could handle the family's many boats.

Her first time at the controls of the jet ski, her mother seated right behind her, Kendra fell in love with water and power. When she turned too quickly and a wave flipped the personal water-craft, dumping both of them into the fifty-degree water in front of their house on Whidbey Island, she developed an immediate respect for the power of water.

At fourteen, she'd learned to sail small Lasers and competed in local regattas. Near her fifteenth birthday The Tall Ships visited Seattle. Her parents had taken their whole family, even purchasing VIP tickets that allowed them to tour the ancient-style vessels. She had pelted the captain and crew with so many questions her parents had to drag her off the ship.

To extend her knowledge and understanding of wind, and to satisfy her need for speed and adrenaline, she secretly signed up to join a yacht racing crew. The owner knew her father and allowed her to literally learn the ropes. At racing time, she sat dockside and cheered them on, too young to be a member of the crew.

By sixteen, she was captaining her parents' large cabin cruiser around Puget Sound, dodging deadheads like a pro. The trees, a leftover from the abundant logging industry, floating vertically in the waters from Seattle to Vancouver, British Columbia, could be extremely harmful to any size boat, even cruise ships.

The summer before her senior year of high school, her father let her chart their path and take the controls for hours at a time through the inside passage on their way to and from Juneau. Because of the numerous islands protecting the Canadian shoreline, the currents and tides were extremely tricky, gushing between islands like a funnel.

Facing down huge wakes thrown from gigantic cruise ships was another challenge for the teenager.

Then there was the relentless westerly wind that had nothing to stop it after leaving Russia. It alone could cause waves as tall as their bow.

Kendra met the challenge and mastered the sea.

She had loved every minute of that vacation. Her brothers had gotten seasick while she stood behind the wheel with a smile on her face riding the swells like a cowgirl on a bucking bronco.

She had the same elation the summer before her junior year at the Naval Academy when midshipmen spent weeks at a time aboard Navy ships. When they were headed into rough weather, she'd asked the commander if she could take the helm for a while.

Commander Thurman raised one eyebrow. "If you think you can handle her, go right ahead. The puke bucket's over there. Puke on my deck, you clean it up, along with the heads."

"Aye aye, sir," she'd said with a knowing grin. Kendra had taken the controls of the amphibious assault ship, slicing through the growing swells like an expert...smiling the entire time. It wasn't her first rodeo. Sure, it was a much bigger ship than her parents' cabin cruiser, but it was also heavier and had more power.

They'd taken water over the helicopter landing deck a few times, but she'd kept the ship steady and sure. Six hours later, after the storm had passed, the commander of the LHD patted her on the shoulder. "Hell of a ride but you handled her better than some of my saltiest sailors." To congratulate her, he'd ranked her number one of all the midshipmen aboard.

By the time she'd made it to the fleet and was assigned to an old LPD, Commander Thurman had been promoted to captain and was the commanding officer of an aircraft carrier. During workup for deployment, she'd run into him at the officers' club, exchanging only a few words. Two days later she'd received orders to report to his aircraft carrier.

Her naval career had taken off like a cruise missile—guided and on target—until it blew up... like her marriage.

"Kendra, are you okay?" Andrew's voice brought her back to the present. "You don't seem to be enjoying the show. Is he repeating too many tricks?"

She shook her head. "No. He's great." She forced a smile, mentally crawling out of the depressing part of her past. She was on a new path. She'd worked hard to reach captain and was proud of the four gold stripes on each shoulder.

Kendra watched Andrew out of the corner of her eye. He wasn't the overzealous, kiss the brass ass, take credit for the work of others like her ex. He would never hold his rank over her.

Andrew would never force her to quit the job she loved because he became her boss. She was so glad Monarch Cruise Line didn't have fraternization rules. She didn't want to give Andrew up. Nor would she ever ruin his possibility for promotion.

He slyly slid his hand to the small of her back, leaning so none of the other staff or crew could see him. "I couldn't stand having you so close and not touch you." He spoke in a low tone rather than a whisper, which would have garnered attention.

Leaning back into him, but not too close, she spoke almost directly into his ear. "Only two more hours."

The crowd erupted with laughter and clapping.

Damn. I missed that one.

Vowing to pay attention, she focused on the rest of the show. For the last act of the evening, the magician had three people from the audience on the stage and a helper on the other side directing people to their seats, helping them as needed.

"I can never figure out how he does this," she said quietly over her shoulder to Andrew.

"You really want to know how?" he asked before he spoiled the illusion for her.

She wasn't sure. There was something mystical about not knowing how a trick was accomplished. She'd seen it several times and was always thrilled and amazed.

Fighting with herself, she finally said, "Yes." Then quickly said no.

Andrew chuckled. "Tell you what. Watch his assistant, not the magician. If you still want me to tell you, ask me later tonight."

"Are you saying it's a diversionary tactic and the magician is the diversion?" Now her interest was piqued.

"Just watch the show." His grin was one of her favorite things.

"Oh, my gosh," she whispered when the magician's helper, totally in the shadows, moved things around. It was still fun to see the conclusion of the trick.

"We used diversionary tactics all the time in the SEALs. 'Look over here while we complete our mission over there.' It's Rescue 101." Andrew shrugged as though it was nothing.

Kendra knew better. SEALs put their lives on the line every time they went out on a mission. She had no idea how many operations he'd been involved in, directly and on the periphery, but she'd seen his list of medals. Impressive, to say the least. That was the only thing that was written on his standard employment form concerning his years of active service. He never talked about his time in the Navy, and she hadn't pried. She wasn't anxious to share either. Maybe someday she'd tell him why she'd resigned her commission. That meant she'd have to tell him about Carter.

Applause and whistles filled the theater.

"I need to run back to the bridge and do the turnover to the night crew." She squeezed his powerful bicep as she walked past.

He leaned over and said in a low tone that sounded like a growl, "My cabin. Tonight."

Guests started pouring up the aisles. She needed to disappear before somebody stopped her. She had an approachable personality, but times like this, she didn't want to play nice with the guests. She had too much left to do before she could meet Andrew and fall asleep in his arms.

"Okay." She scurried all the way to the other end of the ship and up the staff stairs.

An hour later, Kendra had just finished turning the bridge over to Lieutenant Commander Adams for the night watch when Captain Phillips pushed through the glass door.

Oh. Shit.

He wasn't scheduled to be on duty until eight o'clock the next morning.

"Captain Benson, a word, please." He walked into the office on the side of the bridge normally used by officer of the watch to fill out logs or use the computer to check something…most often personal.

Oh. Fucking. Shit.

"Yes, sir." She didn't quite stand at attention, but her spine was straight, prepared for anything he threw at her.

The captain slid behind the computer and logged in. While waiting for everything to come up, he glanced toward the helm chair where Lieutenant Commander Adams sat perched like a king. Returning his gaze to her, he nodded to the door. "Close that and pull the blinds."

Oh, no. Double fucking shit.

Completing her tasks, she turned back to face her superior officer.

"I'm glad I caught you before you left for the night." He ran both hands over his face then massaged his temples. He swore in German before continuing in English. "God, I hate these things."

Kendra braced. No matter what he said, she would keep her face passive. She wouldn't react.

He lifted his gaze and stared at her for a long moment. Letting out a deep breath, he finally spoke. "I have to write the one-month report on Lieutenant Commander Adams." He cocked his head to the side. "I feel I can be honest with you. I don't *like* him, but I want this report to be as honest as possible so I'm hoping you will help balance my personal feelings toward him."

Kendra wanted to laugh. "Sir, I feel I can be honest with you." She repeated his words. "I don't like him either."

The huge captain roared with laughter. Kendra couldn't help but join in. When he finally got himself under control, he spoke again. "If you don't even like him, he's fucked."

That time Kendra laughed so hard tears rolled down her face. "Sir, I'm pretty sure between the two of us we can find some positive attributes. His *need to improve* side will just be longer."

The captain looked up at her and grinned. "I'm not sure there's enough room here for that list."

Half an hour later the captain closed out of his personnel program. Standing, he headed toward the door. "Thank you, Kendra. You're the best staff captain I've ever worked with. You're going to make an excellent ship's master. You know they'll start you out on a smaller ship, most likely one of their lower end lines. You'll do just fine." Before he opened the door, he pointed back to the computer. "Your personnel reports are excellent. I couldn't think of a damn thing for you to improve upon." Before he opened the door he added, "I want you to know that I approve of your relationship with Commander Buchanan.

You're both wonderful officers and I'm proud to serve with you."

This time Kendra wanted to cry for a whole different reason. His words were the opposite of what she'd heard during her final year in the Navy. "Thank you, sir. You'll never know how much that means to me."

She followed him to the officers' cabins, saying good night as he closed the door behind him, the first one on the left. Hers was next in line but after checking the empty hall, she entered Andrew's with the key he'd given her.

Closing the door quietly behind her, she leaned back letting it take all her weight as she absorbed the view of Andrew. Most likely naked under the sheet, he sat leaning against the headboard reading *Sun Tzu: The Art of War*. His bedside table was stacked with biographies of Winston Churchill, Teddy Roosevelt, Robert E. Lee, *Greatest Battles of the Civil War*, and a dozen more nonfiction war-related books.

"Didn't you get enough of that shit at the Academy?" She asked as she stepped forward.

Marking his place with a tattered index card, he closed the book and laid it on top of his stack. "I enjoy reading history. I find the way these men think and reacted to be fascinating. I'd rather read about these than watch mindless television any day. These men were real, faced with real world-changing situations."

Kendra slowly unbuttoned her blouse, shrugging it off her shoulders. It needed to be washed so she simply tossed it aside. Toeing off her sturdy white lace-up shoes at the same time she unzipped her white uniform slacks, she looked down at her basic white bra. She wished she could wear something lacy and sexy, but the damn female uniforms were practically see-through.

Andrew sat there in bed watching her through half-lidded eyes, saying nothing.

She decided to give him a little show by turning around and shimmying out of her slacks, pulling down her plain white underpants at the same time. Standing upright, her back still to him, she unhooked her bra and seductively slid the straps off each shoulder.

Naked, she left her clothes in a heap and walked toward him, caressing her breasts.

He lifted the sheets, and her eyes were drawn to his impressive erection.

"You've been thinking about me." She glanced toward the tall stacks of books. "At least in the last two minutes."

Andrew pulled her into his bed and rolled on top of her. "You teased me with that pretty little ass of yours. What did you expect?"

With his knees between her legs, he shoved them apart, running his fingers through her wet folds. "You've been thinking about me," he repeated her statement.

She looked into his hazel eyes that were more brown now in the basic beige cabin. She wrapped her fingers around his cock and guided him inside her. This was the way she wanted him tonight. Slow, gentle, taking their time. He seemed to understand her need, pulling out almost completely before leisurely sliding back in.

Dropping to his elbows, he ran his fingers through her hair, brushing it away from her face.

"You're so beautiful," he whispered before he dropped his head and kissed her. Like their movements, the kiss was tender, unrushed.

Kendra dragged her fingernails down his spine, and he arched, diving deeper into her. She grabbed his butt cheeks and pulled him further inside. Wanting more, she bowed up and wrapped her legs around his narrow hips, changing the angle and his depth.

He let out a slow ragged breath, inching his knees closer. "Doll, you know I love it when you move this way."

She captured his face in both her hands. "Why do you think I do it?"

"You're so fucking tight tonight but it's so soft." He pulled out then slowly glided in.

She tightened all of her muscles and he hissed in a breath through his clenched teeth.

"Doll, I hope you're close because I'm not going to last much longer if you keep that up."

"Not there yet." She was simply enjoying their connection.

"What's it gonna take to get you there?" She heard the edge of desperation in his voice.

She didn't want him to come without her, but she hated to ask for what she needed. With her hips up in the air, his arms stiff against the mattress, she slid her hand between them and rubbed her clit.

"Holy fuck, that's sexy. I can feel your muscles around me tighten." He gritted his teeth, and she was afraid he was going to come first.

He always made sure that she orgasmed before he did. She could tell he was trying everything he could to wait for her. She rubbed her bundle of nerves harder and faster. When she could hardly catch her breath and her muscles shook, she let herself go.

He stiffened and growled, rolling to the side before he collapsed on top of her. He pulled her sweaty body next to his, nuzzling his nose into her hair.

She wasn't sure if he said a word, or it was a long exhaled breath. Contentedly, she snuggled into his large body. In the next breath, he was asleep. Her body sated, her mind relaxed, she fell into a very deep sleep.

CHAPTER 6

THE NEXT MORNING AS THEY WERE GETTING dressed in their running gear, Andrew laughed at Kendra's running commentary of her conversation with Captain Phillips the night before.

"I'm not surprised he thinks so highly of you." Kendra looked away as though she was hiding something from him. When they stood, he took her in his arms. "Doll, you're wonderful at your job. I don't think I could find a single person on the ship to say anything bad about you, especially in the performance of your duties. Never put yourself down." He leaned in and gave her a quick kiss, knowing if it was longer than that, they would never get out of his bedroom.

As they took the stairs side-by-side, he remembered he was off the next day. "Tomorrow will be my last day off before I leave this ship. How would you like to take an excursion?"

"Don't remind me. You're going to be gone far too soon." They exited the door on the running deck. "I'm not sure if I'll be able to take off. The flu is knocking out the bridge crew so I might need to take extra duty."

"Let me know as soon as you can." Andrew stretched his hamstrings. Perhaps if Kendra couldn't go, he'd see if Holden, Tavis, Keene, and Grant wanted to do something together. He felt bad that he hadn't been able to see much of any of them.

Close to lunchtime, Andrew was walking the deck, checking to be sure there were no disturbances. He saw his friend Grant lying on a lounge next to the woman he'd been with during the magician's show.

"How is everyone going to see my barbaric mark on your fantastic tit if you cover it up with makeup?" Grant said quietly.

"They aren't," the pretty woman next to him pointed out.

"Party pooper," Grant teased.

Andrew's shadow fell over her, and she tipped her head back to look at him. "How's the cruise going so far?"

"Excellent," Grant responded. "Thanks for making sure a beautiful, fun, sexy woman was onboard for my cruise," he teased as he grabbed her hand.

She threaded her fingers with his and looked

at Grant as though he was the best thing since canned beer.

Andrew chuckled. "Yep. I definitely made sure the perfect woman would be onboard for you, Grant. It's part of my job," he joked. "Listen. I don't have a lot of time right now, but I have tomorrow off. We'll be in Costa Rica. Any chance you'd like to do an excursion with me?"

Grant glanced at Callie, probably because he didn't want to leave her out.

"Your friend can come too, of course," Andrew quickly added.

Grant grimaced. "I'm so sorry, Callie, I'd like you to meet my friend, Andrew Buchanan. He is the security officer of the ship. Andrew, Callie." He nodded between the two of them.

She looked at her hand, which was captured in Grant's, unable to shake. "Nice to meet you."

"It's a pleasure to meet you as well." Andrew grinned. "Thank you for entertaining my friend. I was serious about you joining us tomorrow."

Callie waved a hand between them. "Oh, don't worry about me. You don't need a third wheel."

Andrew laughed. "I'm pretty sure I'd be the third wheel. Not you, but one of my coworkers might be off tomorrow too. She might be willing to join us." He still hadn't heard back from Kendra.

"Oh? Coworker? Is this amorous?" Grant asked.

Andrew shrugged. "Maybe." He was grinning though, like a man who certainly hoped it could be more than romantic.

Grant turned back toward Callie. "Did you have plans with Melanie?"

She shook her head. "No. She and Holden are planning to see the sloths. Not going to lie. That sounds kind of boring. I was thinking of something more adventurous. Like zip lining."

Grant grinned. "I like that plan."

"I can easily arrange that," Andrew stated. "I have connections," he joked.

"Let's do it then," Grant agreed.

"Excellent. I'll text you the details in a while. Enjoy the sun but be careful. We're getting very close to the equator and the sun is much more intense." Andrew stared at Grant. "You might need to put some more suntan lotion on the perfect woman." He waved as he walked away, so happy his friends were having such a good time.

The next several hours were filled with routine paperwork, several guests being locked out of their safes, random drug testing of food and beverage personnel, and the report of illegal activity in Costa Rica increasing. None of the latter seemed to involve tourists, mostly local drug dealers.

He was finally able to stop for lunch. Andrew texted Kendra: *Grabbing a late lunch. Did you eat?*

No time. Crazy up here.

Can I bring you something?

UR my guardian angel! Turkey sandwich. Veggie sticks. Chocolate!!

Andrew could have guessed her menu, especially the chocolate. He went through the buffet line filling two trays. He knew what she liked and grabbed several other things as well as her brief list. Minutes later, he unlocked the door to her cabin, and set the food out on her balcony table.

He took a picture of her dining table and sent it to her.

Seconds later her door opened. "You are a godsend." She picked up the sandwich and bit into it before she even sat down. She moaned as though in ecstasy. "I was starving but every time I tried to leave, someone else came in with another problem."

Kendra had the second most important job on the ship. Every officer reported to her, except for Captain Phillips. She was his filter, hearing every problem, solving whatever she had the authority to do, before passing the situation on to the master of the ship. Fortunately, he hadn't needed her that day.

"Take a deep breath and relax. Look at that beautiful turquoise water." Andrew had opted for the chicken and dumplings that day, and he took a bite. This might be one of the last times he'd be able to sit on Kendra's balcony and take solace in the gorgeous Caribbean Sea. He was down to single digits as an employee of Monarch Cruise Lines. He had no idea whether he would take another contract with them or move on to another job altogether.

"Maybe you should take your own advice." She rubbed the crease between his eyebrows with her index finger. "What were you thinking about?"

"I only have nine more days on this contract." He reached across the table and took her hand. "I have no idea what I'm going to do."

"What are your choices?" With her free hand, she picked up a carrot stick and dipped it in the ranch dressing.

Andrew hadn't talked to anyone about his decision. "Well, of course I could take another contract with Monarch, or one of their subsidiaries." He squeezed her hand. "You'll be master of your own ship, but I'm sure it will be on one of their less expensive lines." Monarch owned several cruise line brands: its well-known inexpensive party cruises that often went out only a few days in length, and a midrange line that primarily offered weeklong cruises. Its high end, like the one they were currently on, offered ten- to fourteen-day trips at much higher dollar points.

She squeezed his hand back and held his gaze. "I'd love to serve on board with you again." She glanced away. "But following me would be a demotion. Your next ship should be another one this size."

Returning her gaze to him, she suggested, "Or you can move to another cruise line that carries thousands more guests. I'm sure you'll have excellent personnel reviews from Captain Phillips. You'll be able to get a job anywhere."

It was Andrew's turn to look away. "I'm not sure I want to be a security officer again." He turned back toward her, taking both of her hands in his. "You know I was a SEAL. I miss that adrenaline high." *And knowing that I was doing something important.* "I feel like my true talents and skills are wasted on a cruise ship."

Kendra nodded. "I know. So, what are you thinking? Joining a Beltway bandit like those government contractors? Going back to the sandbox?"

He shrugged. "I don't know. Maybe. Two of the men who used to work for me are forming a company of former SEALs. I don't know a lot about it right now since they're just getting started. Supposedly, they have a contact in the government pretty high up who has promised them contracts." He sighed. "I'm not really sure I want to go to work for men who used to work for me."

"So, I'll repeat my question, what are you thinking?" She took her napkin and dabbed her lips.

"That's just it, I don't know." He held her gaze, nervous about his next question. "Will you come visit me in Miami?"

"Of course. I want to see you away from the ship. Away from our jobs." Her smile brightened his world. "You think we might be able to take that beachside rental for a second month if we decided to? My contract is up in three weeks."

"If not that one, we'll find another one." He knew he was grinning like a doofus. Kendra was going to spend time with him. Weeks, maybe more. "If not Miami, we can go anywhere. I've helped to dock the ship on islands that I've never been able to see."

Kendra laughed. "Take a cruise. What a great idea."

"We'll get off at every port of call and take the most exciting excursions they offer." His words reminded him to ask, "Any chance you can get tomorrow off? I've asked my friend Grant to go zip lining. He's going to bring his...I guess I should call her girlfriend. It sounds nicer than cruise hookup."

"Yes, I'm off. The doc gave everybody on the bridge medicine to keep the rest of us from getting sick." She practically jumped up and down in her seat. "Let's do it!"

The alarm on Kendra's phone went off. She groaned as she stood up. "Sorry, the job calls." She bent down to give him a kiss. When he tried to pull her into his lap, she shoved away. "Now you don't get a kiss until I see you at the end of the shift."

Andrew tore out of his chair and swooped up Kendra, kissing her thoroughly. "That will give you something to think about until midnight."

When her feet touched the floor, she cupped his face. "I think about you all the time." Leaning up, she pecked his lips. "I want you in my bed tonight." She grinned. "I have something special planned. Now you have something to think about until midnight."

He was late getting to her room. A guest in the casino had loudly accused one of the dealers of cheating. The casino concierge couldn't mollify the customer who continued to increase in volume. He'd called for security and since it was on Andrew's way back to his cabin, he stopped in the casino. After reviewing the video footage, he showed it to the guest who finally admitted he was wrong. The casino concierge awarded him onboard credit and a discount off his next cruise, which seemed to pacify the guest.

Texting her on his way upstairs, all he wanted to do was strip off his clothes and crawl in bed with Kendra. He was looking forward to spending the next day with her. When he opened her door, she obviously had other ideas. She laid spread out on her bed in the most see-through negligée he'd ever seen.

Both his brain and his cock sprang to life.

* * *

ANDREW'S internal alarm clock went off shortly before dawn, his normal time to get up to exercise. He made the executive decision for both of them that they were going to skip their morning run. They'd made ravenous love after he'd ripped the sheer lace from her body with his teeth, kissing every inch of exposed skin before sliding into her. Every time they had sex it seemed better than the last.

His phone buzzed.

He grabbed it quickly to look at the caller ID.

Charley.

He snagged his boxers off the floor and quietly stepped outside as the phone vibrated a second time. He slid into his underwear before he sauntered toward the edge of her balcony.

"Good morning, Ms. Charley. This must be very important for you to call me at this hour of the morning." He'd only spoken with the mysterious woman twice before and his current position as security officer was the result. The second time was to tell him to answer the next phone call. As soon as she'd hung up, his phone had rung. The man on the other end had explained that his retirement had been approved with full benefits. As far as he was concerned, she was his guardian angel.

He had no idea who she was, or where either, only that she had some pretty powerful connections. During his brief conversation with Ryker, one of the platoon members he'd sent into Ethiopia, Charley was the one who had put him on the correct path to finding and rescuing his teammates.

As far as Andrew was concerned, he owed this woman.

"I'm sorry I don't have time for small talk, but I hear you're doing well on the cruise ship. I'm sure you're relatively bored but I might be able to cure that. I know you're scheduled to dock in Costa Rica in a few hours. Would you be able to end your contract a few days early?"

Fuck. Even if he could, he really didn't want to. Things were going so well with Kendra. Their future together looked better every day.

"Ma'am, I don't know but as you obviously know, I only have a few days left. Can it wait until we return to Miami?" He was so torn. She pulled him out of the lowest low he'd ever been in in his life. Any other time, he would do anything for this woman.

Charley let out a hum. "I understand. You don't want to fuck things up with Kendra."

How the fuck did she know about his growing relationship with Kendra?

"Tell you what, I'm going to keep you right where you are from now. I want you to be my eyes and ears in that area. We're not sure what's going on. All we know for sure is that the Chinese are up to something and it's huge."

"Yes, ma'am. I've heard rumblings. As I'm sure you know, the fleet strike force is in the Caribbean heading toward the Panama Canal to replace the fleet heading into Seattle." Nothing he'd told her wasn't available on the internet or in the newspapers in Norfolk and Jacksonville. Both had large spreads as the fleet pulled out of port.

"Yeah, I know all that, but things are moving fast. When you dock, the local bow linemen will hand you a satellite phone. Keep it close. It will be programmed with my number. Use it if you see or hear anything unusual."

"Yes, ma'am."

"When you're back in Miami, I may have more work for you. Call if you need me." The line went dead.

He felt a warm hand on his back.

Without looking, he knew it was Kendra.

"Do you have to go to work?" He pulled her into his body and she wrapped the ship's big fluffy robe around them both.

"Not yet." Andrew kissed the top of her head, smiling into her hair. She had no idea what he meant by that. "I've decided we're not going to run this morning. We got plenty of hard pounding exercise last night and today will be very physical. This is our day to spend together." Though he wasn't working, he'd be sure to be at the bow when the lines were tied.

"If we're not going anywhere for hours, let's go back to bed." With her arm around his back, she guided him to her bed. "We don't often get morning sex."

At the mere suggestion, Andrew was hard. He couldn't get enough of this woman.

CHAPTER 7

KENDRA HAD STARTED OFF THE MORNING WITH AN orgasm and a nap followed by breakfast in bed. She'd been married for ten years, dated Carter for two years before that, and never once had he brought her breakfast in bed. She could probably count on one hand how many orgasms she'd had first thing in the morning. Her ex wouldn't do anything in the morning until he'd accomplished the three Ss: shit, shower, and shave. He wouldn't even kiss her until he'd brushed his teeth...and until she'd brushed too.

She'd been dating Andrew for five weeks, or was it six? Maybe it was seven. This man had given her several morning Os and had brought her wake-up treats numerous times. Could this man get any better?

Yes. They were one of the first ones to walk off the ship to a waiting private SUV. No bus

80

where they had to wait for everyone who couldn't find the meeting point or that was habitually late.

She kissed him. Simply because she could. She'd left the ship with zero fanfare. Unless someone had been hanging over their balcony and happened to recognize her wearing dark blue mid-thigh shorts, a nondescript short-sleeve blue blouse, gym shoes, and a blue ball cap, no one knew that she'd left the ship.

Except two of his men on gangplank duty. Just like the guests, she had to scan her badge on the machine before she could leave. Andrew scanned his two friends out at the same time.

"Grant, and Callie, right?" she asked as they walked down the long pier toward the cruise terminal. Vendors were just opening their booths selling small jewelry chests adorned with brightly colored flowers and papier-mâché jungle animal masks.

"Yes, I'm Callie." Kendra shook the young woman's hand.

Extending his hand, he said, "Grant. We met when I first came aboard. I'm honored to have you with us, Captain Benson."

"No titles. Today I'm simply Kendra and he's Andrew."

The handwoven purses, long necklaces of brightly colored beads, and hand-painted gauze dresses caught her attention. "I don't know about you, Callie, but I might need to stop by some of the shops on my way back to the ship."

She didn't often get off the ship while in port, and less often took the time to browse through local crafts. She knew that in the cities the money made off tourists on her ship was the difference between whether some of the local people ate that day or not. Here next to the terminal, the vendors had to pay to sell so close to the ships. She'd look elsewhere for local goods.

Andrew grabbed her hand. "We need to get out of here quickly." He nodded back to the ship where guests were trickling out.

"Let's go."

The forty-minute drive into the mountains was typical of any Third World country. Homes —made from slapped together sheets of used plywood surrounding a dirt floor topped by ridged pieces of tin slanted in one direction— would be considered hovels in the United States. Gardens scratched out of dry dust provided their family's sustenance.

Kendra had to smile at the irony. Most every person carried a cell phone.

The higher they went, the more vegetation there was. Sparse trees soon replaced bushes. As the American-made SUV climbed higher into the mountains, the trees grew taller and thicker, and the road grew thinner. In the middle of the curve, they turned onto a dirt road with tighter bends.

In another few miles, when they finally stopped, Kendra was never so glad to step onto solid ground.

"I can ride a ship through a hurricane force gale, but I almost lost my breakfast coming up the mountain," she confessed.

"Thank God for the air conditioning." Callie grabbed her daypack. "If we had to depend on open windows, I would've been sick for sure."

"Feel sorry for the guests going on this excursion. The bus doesn't have air conditioning." Andrew shook his head. "You can probably blame me for the fast ride. I told the driver we wanted to get here before the crowds. I don't know if you looked around this morning, but there were two more ships pulling into port."

"Then let's get going." Kendra headed for the open door to the small store. Since Andrew had made the arrangements, she let him and Grant handle the payment. She'd pay him back in a very personal way later that evening. Meanwhile, she browsed the locally made crafts.

"More in here." A woman in a T-shirt bearing the company name pointed to another section of the building. Kendra followed her through the very small door. Her eyes were instantly drawn to the gauzy dresses, each unique in its color combinations. She lifted several off the hanging rack and held them against her body.

"I like the one with all the blue colors." Andrew walked up behind her.

"That's my favorite, too, but I'm not sure it's going to fit."

"You try on." The woman pointed to a door leading outside. "Ba...Batum." Kendra must have had a confused look on her face because Andrew stepped in and started speaking Spanish to her. The only word Kendra recognized was *baño*, the Spanish word for bathroom.

"She said that you can try on the dress in the bathroom, which is out back around the corner. She asked me to have you put it on over your head so that it doesn't touch the floor." Andrew grimaced. "I'll walk out there with you."

Once they were outside, he confessed, "I have no idea how bad these bathrooms are. I do see that they have running water, though. Keep in mind, the cruise line wouldn't bring our guests here if they hadn't already approved of this place."

To her relief, the bathroom had American-style toilets and community porcelain sinks.

"You might want to use the facilities while you're here," he suggested. "I doubt there's any place to go once we head deeper into the woods, unless you want to use a tree. I wouldn't suggest that option. Costa Rica has all kinds of poisonous shit: viper snakes, poisoned tree frogs. They even have this thing called the Brazilian wandering spider."

"Enough." Kendra held up her flat palm toward him. She glanced around and back to the partial door that was barely long enough to hide someone sitting on the commode.

As though he could read her mind, he reassured her, "I'll be right here if you want to model it for me. I'll make sure nobody can see you." He leaned in and whispered, "That body is mine and I don't share."

She kissed him quick then stepped into the plywood stall. Hanging her backpack on the hook, she placed each piece of clothing on top of it, so nothing touched the wet floor. The moment the lightweight material slid over her skin she knew she'd buy it. It fit loose, but that's the way she'd seen it worn in ports throughout the Caribbean.

She stripped out of the dress and put her clothes back on while using the facilities. She flushed, thankful that the plumbing worked, and stepped out to the common area where both men and women washed their hands.

"Give me a minute to go buy this then I'll be ready to climb to the first zip line."

When she entered the shop, she walked straight over to Callie. "You might want to go use the bathroom now. There aren't any once we get started."

"Good idea."

Without Kendra suggesting it, Grant followed her out.

A few minutes later, her purchase tucked away in her backpack, all four stood in front of a tall young man who looked to be about twenty. "I think this should fit you." He handed her a harness then passed out three more. Holding one in front of himself, he explained, "Step into it like you would a pair of shorts."

By the time he'd finished his sentence, all four of them were adjusting the straps to fit their thighs and waist. Straps with large carabiners were attached to a thick rope pulled tight overhead between two trees. Without instruction, she clipped one onto her harness and sat down, tightening her straps. When she looked to the side, Andrew was doing the same. On her other side, Grant was helping Callie.

The young man stood in front of Kendra and started to reach between her belt and thigh straps to unhook her harness from the hanging rope.

Andrew growled. "I'll check her." He practically shoved their guide out of the way. Grant was already checking Callie's and at his sideways glance, the young man walked on past.

Andrew tugged on each thigh strap and her belt. "You've done this before." It was a statement, not a question.

"You aren't the only adrenaline junkie." She

leaned forward and gave him a quick kiss. "Be good. He's the one who knows where the zip lines are."

"I'm positive I can get us out of here." He chuckled. "Once we start at the first line, they're all connected. The only way to go is down."

"Who's going first?" Andrew asked as they approached the first line.

Kendra hip-butted him. "Me. That way I can take video and laugh at you from the next platform."

Andrew growled, standing at his full height, pulling his shoulders back. "Why on earth would you think I might be funny?" he joked. "Do you know how many times I've done something like this without the safety harnesses in a dangerous war zone?"

Kendra glanced at Callie and watched her swallow. Andrew was revealing things she didn't know if he wanted Grant's girlfriend to hear. She knew, and most likely Grant did also. Hell, Grant may have been with him when they were forced to zip line. She wondered how often he and his fellow SEALs used this method to make a fast escape.

Grant gave Andrew a playful shoulder shove. "No shop talk. We're here to have fun."

Kendra held up both hands. "My bad. But I'm still taking videos. Of all three of you. So, just remember, later I'll be comparing which one of you was most freaked out."

Grant chuckled. "It's not going to be me."

"Me neither," Andrew agreed.

They both looked at Callie.

She gave them an eye roll. "I love zip lining. This isn't my first rodeo."

Andrew reached out and snagged Kendra's phone out of her hand. "It's decided then."

"What's decided?" she asked, trying to snatch it back.

Andrew stepped in front of her. "I'm going first. I'll take the videos of *you*."

Kendra shook her head. "No way. I already called it. You can't switch the rules."

Callie and Grant slowly shook their heads. Everyone was enjoying the relaxed atmosphere between the four of them.

Andrew slid her phone into his pocket as he clipped onto the first line. "Wait until I get my gloves off before you start." He jumped off the ledge and spread his arms wide, lying back in the harness. Slowing his speed when he got close to the platform, he landed gently. After unhooking and removing his leather gloves, he clipped into the safety wire around the tree and took out her phone. "Ready."

"I want my phone back when I get there." She clipped on, jumped, and posed as though she were casually sitting in a chair with her legs crossed at the knee until just before she slowed to land. *This is so much fun!*

For the rest of the day, they took turns taking videos, each trying to outshine the others' poses. As they finally walked the short distance down to the store, Kendra had laughed so much her cheeks hurt.

"I'm going to grab waters for everyone," Grant announced as soon as he stepped out of his harness.

"No need." Andrew handed all four harnesses to their guide along with the tip. "Cold beer is waiting for us in the SUV." He pointed to where their driver sat with the vehicle running. Several older buses were parked next to it. A few people milled around, but it looked as though most were already on the course.

"Perfect timing," she said as she slid her arm around Andrew's waist. "And thanks for thinking about the cold beer. I could really use one about now." She glanced toward the back of the store. She could wait an hour to get back on the ship and use her own private bathroom.

Kendra sighed as soon as she sat down in the SUV. He must've been running the air conditioning for quite a while since the vehicle was cool compared to the hot steamy jungle. The driver immediately handed her a cold local beer. She twisted off the cap and downed about a third.

The trip back to the ship seemed so much

faster. She asked the driver to drop them off in town as they all got out and walked around Limón. She loved the brightly colored buildings. The shop owners seemed to prefer bright yellows and lime green mixed with blues and reds. Entire pink buildings that looked to be plucked out of the French Quarter of New Orleans dotted the main street. Like many other Caribbean countries, many painted their buildings the color of the ocean in turquoise and pastel green.

"Mind if I drop into some of the shops?" Kendra asked the group.

"I'd love to go in that one." Callie pointed to the next one down the street. None of the shops had doors. Merchandise spilled out into the street from open fronts. Every inch of space on the tables and underneath was filled.

Callie picked up a hand-carved bowl that showed the many layers of the wood including the rough bark along the edge. "You can't find anything like this back in the U.S." She turned the bowl over and over, caressing the smooth wood.

Kendra plucked up a box that was made of multiple kinds of wood cleverly pieced together in a starburst design. When she went to pick up the lid, it didn't open. The storekeeper rushed over and showed her that it was really a 3-D puzzle with a secret compartment inside.

"These are so clever. I need to pick up several for my nieces. They'll love these." She took the next ten minutes searching the shapes. She giggled when she spotted an iguana-shaped box. Turning, she wanted to share the story with Andrew.

"One winter I went with my sister and her two daughters to a resort between Cancún and Playa Del Carmen. My niece, who was in her early twenties, was walking back through the paths to her condo one night when this big iguana fell out of a tree onto her head. She whacked it away and it lay on the ground, not moving. Now mind you, this place thought a lot of their iguanas. They had signs with their names on them because they didn't seem to leave that particular area. So, she came running to our condo and we all took flashlights wandering around this area in the middle of the night looking for this fucking iguana. We never found it. Neither did the groundskeepers who were looking for it every time as we passed the next day."

Kendra held up the iguana box. "She needs this."

"You're evil." He pulled her into a hug and kissed her temple. "But that's part of your charm."

They shopped for several blocks then turned and walked down the other side, fascinated by the variety of items each store sold. The closer they got to the pier, the nicer the shops. Stores started to have glass windows instead of open walls. The shopkeepers wore American professional clothing rather than local traditional. Jewelry stores affiliated with the cruise lines packed both sides of the street just before the terminal.

Kendra was almost sad as they walked the final block. It was as though their wonderful day together had ended. She couldn't remember the last time she did something exciting with friends. As they said goodbye to Callie and Grant after scanning their badges to get back on the ship, it seemed so final.

Alone in the staff elevator that took Kendra and Andrew from the fourth deck up to their rooms, he put his arm around her. "That was such a great day. Thank you for going with us."

"I can't remember the last time I had that much fun. I think it's been years since I've gone out with friends. Even when I'm between contracts, I don't have good friends like yours." The elevator opened and they separated slightly until they reached their rooms.

"I stink. I'm going to take a shower and change my clothes." Andrew nodded toward his room. "What do you think about getting a drink at the bar and bringing it up here?"

Kendra grinned at her lover. "I think it would be wonderful if you took a shower and got dressed, then went down to the bar and got us both a drink and brought it up here. I just want to slide into comfy pajamas after I shower and wash my hair."

He looked up and down the hallway, then pulled her in for a kiss. "I'll be back in about twenty minutes. You know you don't need to bother putting on pajamas. They're just going to come off as soon as we're done with our drinks." He stepped back and raised his eyebrows. "Unless you have another number like the one the other night. In that case, we'll skip the drinks."

She shoved him toward his room. "You'll just have to wait and see."

CHAPTER 8

AT FOUR O'CLOCK IN THE MORNING, ANDREW'S phone buzzed. He'd expected the text. In the past three months he'd gone through the entire Panama Canal from the Atlantic to the Pacific Ocean and back three times and he'd done this half canal trip nearly a dozen.

The text indicated the bridge had gotten permission to enter the causeway.

"Well, the check cleared." It was a running joke between bridge crews who crossed through the canal on a regular basis. Every vessel, from a rowboat to an aircraft carrier, had to pay the Panamanian government for the right to pass through the locks. Large cargo ships could pay upwards of half a million dollars. Cruise ships had to pay extra for each cabin no matter whether crew or guest. Andrew didn't want to think about how much had been paid for his trips through the canal.

Kendra yawned as the ship changed course. "We must be coming out of Limón Bay into the channel." Kendra stretched out her arms, pushing him off the bed. "Time to go to work."

He stood and padded naked to the shower. Andrew knew he had exactly twelve minutes left before he had to be down at the waterline door to check the ID of the local pilot and whoever else the Panamanian government decided to send this time. The last trip they crossed all the way through to the Pacific, health inspectors came aboard insisting on seeing the passengers' and crews' COVID shot records. Thankfully the cruise line kept strict records and they were permitted to move forward through the locks. Another time, the transit vessel inspector came aboard and walked every foot of the ship before giving his approval.

Each time, the master of the ship had to present any paperwork they requested. Even though Kendra was not the master, as staff captain she handled most of the paperwork and was required to be right beside Captain Phillips during the inspections.

With a towel wrapped around his narrow waist, Andrew lightly smacked Kendra's exposed bare ass. "Come on, doll. You have to get up too."

"Five more minutes." She groaned and rolled over.

He quickly dressed then rousted her one more time before he kissed her cheek and walked out the door.

In the stairway down to the third deck forward, the satellite phone in his pocket rang.

"Buchanan."

"Chinese moved troops and ships blanketing the shore from Fozou to Hong Kong." Charley skipped any platitudes and jumped into the bad news. "That puts them only three hundred miles from Okinawa, Japan. The United States still has nearly 30,000 active duty military from all four branches of the armed services living on Okinawa. We are now convinced they're going to make a run on Taiwan, most likely in the next twelve hours. I can see that your ship is headed toward the causeway. The fleet strike force is steaming hard and is expected to pass through the locks tonight. You may possibly see them on your way back through."

"What is it you want me to do?" Andrew couldn't imagine what he as a security officer on a cruise ship could do, but if Charley needed him, he'd find a way to do it.

"Same as yesterday. Keep your eyes open for anything out of the ordinary. Be ready if I need you."

"Yes, ma'am."

"Keep this phone with you at all times." In typical Charley style, the line went dead. No *goodbye*. No *good luck*. Just empty air.

A minute later, on Andrew's signal, the side door was opened, and the small metal platform was extended. He could see the pilot boat accelerating to keep pace with the ship and closing in. The first man to leap aboard was wearing military camouflage, and a machine gun strapped on his back. He immediately pulled the weapon across his chest, resting his hand on the receiver, fractions of an inch from the trigger. The pilot came next, followed by another armed military man.

"Our government has demanded I be protected," the man said in near perfect English. "As you may know, the Chinese are on the move. What you may not know is that China is the second largest user of this canal. That container ship in front of you flies the flag of China." He shook his head and handed Andrew his identification papers. "Politics." He then smiled. "Is Captain Phillips still in command?"

"You bet." Although this was the third time this same pilot had boarded, Andrew still compared the picture to the one sent to him from corporate. "Everything seems to be in order. Follow me to the bridge." He signaled for two of his guards to follow them up. Normally, he only left one guard on the bridge, but he thought it wise to maintain a balance. He had several other duties to perform during the lock crossing. There were a lot of moving parts that the guests never really saw.

As soon as the six men stepped onto the bridge, the tension became instantly palpable. "Captain Phillips, Captain Benson, a word, please." Andrew stepped into the glass office and closed the door as soon as the two senior officers entered. "The armed guards are for the protection of the pilot, or so he said. I'm not sure if you two have heard, but China has moved military troops along the coastline from Hong Kong north. They've also moved their fleet into the area just off Taiwan."

Captain Phillips swore in German, shaking his head. "We don't need another war. COVID shut down our industry for nearly two years. A war on the water...we might not recover."

Kendra looked through the glass at the bridge. "I'm really not comfortable with them out there and none of us are allowed to be armed." Her hand dropped to her hip where in the Navy, she carried her pistol.

"Please, be aware of your surroundings," Andrew warned. "I'm leaving two men here. They're very good. One is former Mossad and the other was in the Norwegian Special Forces. They'll be keeping a close eye on all three of them." He focused his attention on the master.

"Sir, you've been through this routine several times. If the pilot does anything, and I mean anything, out of the ordinary, hit the button and I'll come running. Just in case, I'm going to pass out the tasers."

Kendra's eyes grew large.

Andrew held up his hands and spread his fingers wide. "It's just a precaution. The Chinese government is thousands of miles away stomping its feet and beating their spears against their chests." He pasted on a smile, trying to show more confidence than he felt. "We're going to give our guests a wonderful experience in the Panama Canal so they can check that off their bucket lists."

"We need to get out there." Captain Phillips reached for the door but before he opened it, he turned back to Andrew. "I'm damn glad you're my security officer." He opened the door and all three exited.

Andrew had to go to both the bow and the stern of the ship to check the tugboats. He wondered if they, too, had armed military men aboard. There was no way to tell unless they blatantly stood on deck. A glance through his binoculars confirmed that the canal was taking the Chinese threat seriously. He wondered, though, how prepared the Panamanian military truly was. Hopefully, he'd never have to find out.

He considered the appearance of military

grade weapons aboard his ship and throughout the canal as report worthy. Since he was close to his cabin, he went there to make his call.

Kendra's name appeared on his phone when it rang. "You said to report anything unusual," she started without even a hello. "Well, the new Cocoli locks are having trouble closing so all the larger ships entering from and exiting to the Pacific are backed up."

"Do they have any idea what's causing it?"

"We heard two different stories," she explained. "It might be an electrical malfunction."

"And the other?" Andrew encouraged.

Kendra giggled. "It might be a dead crocodile wedged in the pocket that the huge concrete gates slide into."

Andrew chuckled and ran his large hand down his face. "Not that we need to go there, but let's hope it's only a dead croc." For half a second, he wondered how they would remove the large carcass. He shrugged. Not his problem. Not today.

Keeping it professional, he simply answered *thanks* and hung up.

Charley answered on the fourth ring. "Interesting or do I need to send the cavalry. What do you have?"

"Interesting coincidences."

"There are no such things in *our* world as coincidences. Give me all the details." As usual, she was to the point, but her voice sounded tired.

Andrew reported as succinctly as possible. It sounded as though Charley had her hands full.

"Thanks. Stay in touch if you learn anything new." Once again, the line went dead.

Andrew had plenty of his own duties to attend to while transiting the canal.

"Good morning, ladies and gentlemen. I'm Gerald Kaminski, your announcer as we pass through the Panama Canal. I gave the presentation in the theater yesterday afternoon. For those of you who missed it, it's available in your cabin on the lecture channel. I gave a brief overview of what's going to happen today. Now, I'm going to guide you through this unique experience." Andrew always enjoyed Dr. Kaminski's play-by-play. Each time it was a little different and every time he learned something new. Since this might be his last time transiting the locks, he made a point of listening more carefully.

"As you can see, the container ship in front of us is veering to the right. It will be entering the original locks that are over a hundred years old. They were completed in 1914 by the Americans after being originally started in 1881 by the French who gave up digging a canal connecting the Atlantic Ocean with the Pacific. When the Americans took over, they realized the potential problems of connecting the two oceans, so an engineer had the brilliant idea to flood the mountains creating a lake that is eighty-two feet above sea level. This also solved the problem of digging a trench at sea level through tall mountains. There were already rivers running out of both sides that could be deepened and widened to accommodate the vessels of that time."

The announcer continued, "Since our ship is much larger than anything made back in the nineteenth century, we will be transiting the new locks, called the Agua Clara here on the Caribbean side. These were just completed in 2016. The Pacific side has exactly the same configuration; a narrow set of locks and a wide set called the Cocoli. This more than doubled the number of ships that no longer are forced to go all the way around the end of South America to get to the other ocean, saving ships several weeks. About 14,000 ships transit the Panama Canal each year. That's about forty ships a day."

Andrew could hear the ooohs and aahs of the guests who all clung to the rail, many in the bow yet several hundred preferred their private balconies. Part of his job was to watch everybody, stopping anyone who leaned over too far or did something dangerous.

"Upon exiting the third lock, we will be entering Lake Gatún, where anyone taking an excursion will be transported ashore in one of our lifeboats, so please don't panic when you see the crew lowering the lifeboats. The ship will hold in Lake Gatún until we have permission to return through the same three Agua Clara locks. Those on excursions will not be on board during that return trip. They will be picked up in Colón. By the way, since the United States controlled the Panama Canal until 1999, the U.S. dollar is the currency of Panama."

And they'd love for you to spend as much as possible while on your excursion. Andrew had become very cynical after his years in the Navy.

"As we're now approaching the first lock, you are about to enter one of the seven manmade wonders of the world. These locks are one hundred eighty feet wide and one thousand feet long. As soon as the stern tugboat clears the gates, they will be closed, and the water will start to fill the sealed chamber. We'll do this two more times before we're released into Lake Gatún. Coming from the Atlantic side, it's a very short distance to the lake. Ships entering from the Pacific side must maneuver through narrow passageways and around several islands on the lake before they reach these locks."

Moving from bow to stern, port to starboard, Andrew looked for anything out of the ordinary. As usual, the canal hands moved efficiently, securing the cruise ship so it stayed in the middle of the second lock. Guests moved around the ship to get a different view, but no one caused trouble. They were too fascinated by the operation of the world-famous engineering marvel.

"The concrete gates behind us are closed," Dr. Kaminski's voice blasted throughout the ship as many guests watched from their cabin balconies. "As soon as they are shut tight, water will start to fill our lock which is now like a concrete box. As soon as the water level reaches the same height as that in lock number two, the front gates will open, and we will proceed forward."

It took several hours for the ship to pass through all three locks. Andrew stayed busy watching the linemen, and their armed guards, on both sides of the ship. At times, the ship was only mere feet from the men who secured it to the sides of the concrete locks. Most of the time the men carrying guns looked bored.

"As we enter the third lock, you'll notice a large container ship is entering the first lock. We will exit this lock into Lake Gatún completely before it is sealed into the second lock."

As their ship moved smoothly into the lake, Andrew released a long sigh. He had been hyper-aware since the morning phone call from Charley. He watched as groups of guests either went to eat, returned to their cabin, or moved to the stern of the ship to take exiting pictures. He was always surprised at what guests decided was picture worthy. He wondered what people actually did with them once they were home. With the onboard Wi-Fi available, many guests had no doubt already uploaded dozens of lock pictures.

Everyone seemed to behave themselves, so he decided to head back to the bridge to see if the canal controllers had given them a return time to go back through.

Bright light flashed.

Andrew whipped around toward the locks.

A loud boom like he hadn't heard since leaving the war zone focused his gaze on the container ship in lock number two.

The blast wind rocked the ship.

People fell over as the ship righted itself. In the blink of an eye, people had their cell phones out recording the plume of smoke that billowed into the air.

There seemed to be a great deal of activity on board the container ship. Andrew lifted the binoculars that still hung around his neck and focused on the burning ship.

There was no fire.

Just hundreds of armed Chinese military fast roping down the sides to the lock control buildings.

Automatic gunfire ensued.

Andrew was absolutely helpless to do anything but watch the slaughter of dozens of Panamanian canal workers.

Fuck. The bridge.

Andrew took off at a full sprint.

CHAPTER 9

Before Andrew reached the bridge, there were several more blasts but since he was pounding his way down the hall, yelling at people to clear a path, he had no idea of the direction of the explosions.

At the top of the stairs Andrew stopped. Depending where people were standing on the bridge, someone might see him through the glass in the bridge door if he opened the staff stair door.

He cracked it a fraction of an inch, just enough to peek one eye.

Dammit. He couldn't see anyone on the bridge. Not even a shadow.

Opening the door enough so he could slither through and plaster himself against the wall, he made sure the heavy-duty door closed with only a whisper. He bent and crab crawled under the window to the bridge so he could get a better angle. Peeping in, he saw that the two men who entered with the pilot had their guns pointed at Captain Phillips.

His men each had their tasers pointed at a Panamanian soldier.

Andrew needed to get in there and deescalate the tension on the bridge. He needed to enter in full view of his men, so he crawled back under the window and crossed to the other side of the ship. Opening the door without a sound, with the soldiers' backs to him, he stepped in and immediately hand signaled to his men.

"Did any of you see that container ship blow up?"

The soldiers spun their heads and guns toward him.

Both of his men pulled the trigger, sending the taser points directly into their targets. Within seconds the soldiers were writhing on the floor. In one large step, his guards grabbed the guns and had them pointed at the soldiers' heads.

Andrew quickly took the pilot down to the floor, face first, his hands behind his back. He had zip ties around the man's wrists then grabbed his ankles, lashing them together before moving to the jerking and drooling soldiers.

"Kendra, what the fuck happened here?" He knew she would give the most precise accounting.

"We were moving into our hold position when the first bomb went off. The percussive wave rocked the ship. The soldiers obviously didn't have sea legs and stumbled. They must've thought we did it on purpose and pointed their guns at Captain Phillips. Your men immediately pulled their tasers and aimed them at the soldiers. The pilot spoke to the soldiers in Spanish, but I couldn't understand them. I don't believe Captain Phillips could either." Kendra looked at each bridge officer. "Did any of you understand what they'd said?"

Everyone shook their heads.

The pilot rolled over onto his back and sat up. "As she said, they thought you had rocked the ship on purpose. They are very young, inexperienced soldiers who were awakened in the middle of the night and brought to the locks to protect us pilots. Neither of these two had ever even been on a ship." He glanced at the soldiers before returning his gaze to Andrew. "What are you going to do with them?"

"Put them in the brig." It was an answer to the pilot's question as much as an order to his men.

He had a dozen questions for the pilot but waited until the soldiers were off the bridge. "What are your orders?"

"Same as always, coordinate with the fore and aft tugboats to get you into position in each lock, make sure they keep you straight from one lock to the next, then guide you into Lake Gatún so you can anchor close to the dam. We always anchor cruise ships over here because it's close to the marina where you can dock your lifeboats and they can get the buses close."

Andrew had done a lot of interrogating during his time as a SEAL. The man seemed to be telling the truth. Besides, they needed him. He knew the lake.

"Do you know if the locks received any threats in the last twenty-four hours?"

The pilot shook his head. "If they did, they wouldn't tell me. I'm just a local pilot. I wondered if they weren't overreacting, but it seems as though calling out the Army was necessary." He held Andrew's gaze. "Did you say the bombs were on that Chinese container ship?"

"All I know is that a plume of smoke came from the container ship." He wondered how much he could say in front of the pilot. "Captain Phillips, Captain Benson, a word, please." His gaze returned to the pilot. "Navigate us to the usual holding spot."

Once again, the three of them went into the glass office.

"What aren't you telling us?" Kendra asked as soon as the door closed.

"Shortly after the explosion, hundreds of armed Chinese soldiers threw ropes over the side of the ship and started shooting Panamanian soldiers and lock workers." Andrew wasn't going to sugarcoat it. "This is an act of war against the Panamanian government."

He knew he'd better call Charley fast. Given how many cruise guests were taking videos of the explosion, and most likely posting them to every social media possible, she probably already knew. Andrew also knew what he wanted to do next.

"Sir, with your permission, I want to take one of the lifeboats and check if we can still get out on the Pacific side. I have no idea where the other explosions came from."

"Sir, I'm going with him," Kendra announced. "As master of this ship, you are responsible for all the souls aboard. As a former Navy officer, I'll be of more help to Andrew. That way I can stay with the boat if he has to go overland to get a better look."

"Excellent idea." Captain Phillips glanced to his bridge. "I'm not sure what to do next."

"Drop anchor. Act as if none of this ship's plans have changed," Kendra said with authority.

The three of them stepped back onto the bridge.

"Prepare the lifeboats as though we're going to take people ashore for their excursions. We're going to pretend as though nothing is wrong," Captain Phillips announced to the bridge crew.

"Sir, we can't send people ashore until we know what's happening back there." Lieutenant

Commander Adams stood in front of Captain Phillips with his hands on his hips.

"Lieutenant Commander, I do know what's happening back at the locks. I am the one who is responsible for every person on this ship, and I do not take that obligation lightly." He looked over at Andrew and Kendra. "That's why Captain Benson and Commander Buchanan are the only ones leaving the ship in a lifeboat. But we want all our guests to believe that everything will be fine."

"You're going to lie to our guests?" Lieutenant Commander Adams huffed.

"Hell, yes." Kendra got in his face. "The last thing we need is a ship full of people panicking, guests and staff. We want to keep them doing normal things."

Captain Phillips picked up the ship wide intercom. "Ladies and gentlemen, this is Captain Phillips coming to you from the bridge. It looks as though there was a little excitement at the locks but we're not going to let that disturb our enjoyment of today. Everyone going on an excursion, please check your ticket at this time for the meeting place. While the crew gets the lifeboats ready to tender you to the marina to meet your buses for your excursions, I suggest that you enjoy an early lunch. Please meet at your designated time and place for your excursion. For those staying on board, it may be several hours before we are assigned our return time to go back through the locks. We'll keep you informed."

"Excellent job," Andrew told his boss. "We're going to go change while they lower our lifeboat." And Andrew would make that call to Charley.

As soon as she answered, this time it was Andrew who started to speak. He quickly explained what he saw and told her his plan.

"I want to be the first one to know whether the locks are open or closed. The fleet is still heading your way. If they need to be turned around, the sooner the better." She gave orders like a senior military officer. Since he'd never met Charley, he had no idea who she was or how she was so connected.

"Yes, ma'am." Andrew quickly put on an old pair of camouflage utilities and combat boots. He strapped on his personal knives and grabbed several other things that he thought might come in useful.

As they stepped back onto the bridge to check on the progress of the lifeboat, the pilot spoke up once again. "I think it would be a good idea if I went with you," he suggested. "I can show you how to get to places where you won't be seen yet you can get in close to the locks."

Andrew thought about it for a moment and realized they had no paper charts of Lake Gatún since everything on the cruise ship was computerized. True, the lifeboats didn't draft much, but they also didn't have a depth finder and he would need to get close to shore.

He walked over to the pilot still lying on the floor, unsheathed the knife strapped to his thigh, and cut the pilot's ties. His guards had returned from the brig and handed Andrew one of the rifles and extra magazines they'd obviously taken from the soldiers.

"We now have U.S. government permission for this reconnaissance mission," he reassured Captain Phillips.

"You're our security officer. You can't leave us," Lieutenant Commander Adams whined.

"I can and I'm going." Andrew turned and left the bridge with Kendra and the pilot behind him. In the stairwell, he looked over his shoulder and asked, "You're Nigel Perez, right?" He remembered from inspecting the paperwork and ID when they'd picked him up in Limón Bay.

"Yes. And you are the security officer but I don't know your name. Or yours, ma'am."

"I'm Captain Benson and this is Commander Buchanan."

"Nigel, do you have a cell phone?" Andrew asked.

"Yes, would you like to borrow it? My plan has excellent reception in this area." He held his phone out to Andrew.

"No. Who is the highest-ranking person in your government you know?" Andrew asked.

"That would be my boss." His answer echoed up several sets of stairs.

"Call and tell him what happened. The soldiers threatened the life of the master of the ship and as security officer, following international naval law, I threw them in the brig." Andrew wanted to make sure that Nigel had the story straight.

When they reached the fourth deck, the tender platform had been locked in place and a lifeboat was headed down the side of the ship.

When it was tied to the platform, the young seaman stuck his head out of the hatch.

"Thank you for bringing us the boat." Kendra said as she started to board. "Your services are no longer needed here. Report to your chief."

"Yes, ma'am." The young man released a long slow breath before he scurried inside.

As soon as all three were on board, Kendra immediately took the controls and yelled through the window, "Cast off." She glanced at Nigel and Andrew over her shoulder. "Life vests are under that seat. Put them on. Nigel, here beside me. Commander Buchanan needs to take a look at both the older Gatún locks on this side and get a few pictures. We'll then check out the new Agua Clara locks before heading all the way over to the Pacific side."

Andrew immediately stepped into the open hatch. Lifeboats were made to be completely sealed should they need to be used in rough seas. Today, he needed to find the best vantage point possible, which might mean sitting on the bow cover.

"Use the ship to hide your exit and head for that island. Commander, when you go ashore, work your way to the tip of that island. You'll be about fifteen hundred feet from the exit of the original Gatún lock. The foliage should provide you enough coverage that hopefully the Chinese won't see you, yet you should have an unobstructed view of what's happening there.

"Call me on my phone and let me know what you see. We're close enough to use the ship's Wi-Fi in case they're monitoring cell phone calls. I'll report your findings back to the bridge." Kendra in command mode was impressive. He was so damn proud of her. He had to tell her that, when this was over.

What Nigel had called a single island was really several clumped together. Kendra maneuvered the little boat as close to the end as she could without being seen but bright orange boats were hard to camouflage in green vegetation. "Have you had your malaria shots?" she asked.

Andrew looked over his shoulder at her. "I've had every shot imaginable. As a SEAL I was in and out of equatorial countries multiple times." He grinned at her. "Are you really concerned about me, doll?"

Kendra's eyes slid to Nigel before returning to his and softening. "Always."

Andrew jumped off and made his way to the very end of the island.

Hiding behind the last few trees, he had a clear view through his binoculars to both lanes of the Gatún locks. A huge container ship that filled the middle lock seemed to be sinking. Wisps of smoke puffed here and there but Chinese in full uniform were evenly spaced down both sets of locks. Nothing was coming through those as long as armed Chinese guards stood sentinel.

None of the lock personnel in their distinct blue uniforms, or their Panamanian guards, moved. Their unmoving bodies were being tossed into the locks. Crocodiles thrashed in battle over each new body, turning the water crimson.

Andrew snapped several pictures, zooming in on everything he could. He even held his phone camera up to the binoculars for better pictures. As the Chinese soldiers picked up and threw another lock attendant into the water, he switched to video mode to record the international crime.

Unfortunately, he couldn't see the new Agua Clara locks from the island. They were hidden back into the land. He moved as fast as he could through the thick brush back to the lifeboat since they were on a tight schedule.

Pulling out his phone, he checked to be sure he was still connected to the ship's Wi-Fi. *Yes.* He hit speed dial for Kendra. After giving her a full report, he then called Charley and told her what he'd found.

"We're moving a satellite as fast as we can so we can see your location. That process is taking time. Be quick when you look at the new locks. The Cocoli locks on the Pacific side are less than one mile from the U.S. Embassy in Panama City. They heard an explosion and immediately locked down the ambassador. If the Chinese are intending to spread out, we need to stop them immediately."

Andrew burst through the trees and leapt onto the lifeboat, tapping its hood twice as a signal for Kendra to move out. While the boat was underway, he crawled inside.

"There are two smaller islands on the other side of this but to stay hidden, follow the back side." Nigel was expertly directing her to keep them all safe. "You'll have about a thousand feet of open space, but it will bring you into the back. I suggest you go to the far side and follow the edge until you're almost to the front then you have another thousand feet to the second small island. It has a much better view of the Agua Clara locks."

"Thanks, Nigel." Andrew slapped him on the

shoulder. "You were right to insist that you come along."

"I want to find out who has attacked my country...or if it's a coup."

"Is that a possibility?" Kendra asked.

Nigel chuckled. "It's always a possibility. Our last elections were extremely close. Our new president, Sanchez, only won by two percent, ousting the incumbent. He was a bad man. Sanchez promised to curb corruption and deepen ties with China."

"That's going to piss off the United States," Andrew said from behind his binoculars.

"The last president already did that when he established formal ties with the communist country." Nigel continued. "China has become the second-largest user of the canal, especially after the failed attempt of China to work with Nicaragua to build a new canal."

"I heard something about that." Kendra hugged the shoreline, driving the little boat like it was a Grand Prix racecar. "There was a Chinese billionaire who was putting up the money until he lost all his in the market."

"Yes. They dug out quite a bit of it." Nigel pointed so Kendra could see where she was supposed to head. "Probably someday another billionaire will come along and finish it."

"He'll have to crawl in bed with that devil himself, Ortega, or wait until somebody kills the asshole." Andrew had been in Nicaragua more than once on top secret missions. He'd seen for himself the progress on their canal.

Nigel laughed. "Many have tried but no one has yet succeeded." He pointed to where Kendra should turn.

"Saddle up, big boy. Time to take a run." Kendra slowed the boat down and ran it up on a dirt shore behind an outcropping since there were no trees to hide it under.

This island was barely above water, but Nigel had been right, it had an excellent view of the new locks. He moved through the tall grasses, glad he'd worn boots. He prayed no crocodiles lived on this island. Three minutes later he was jogging back toward the lifeboat, pictures uploading to both Kendra and Charley.

As soon as he was aboard, Kendra hit the gas. "We've got a long trip to the other side, make yourself comfortable. It's almost thirty-five miles."

CHAPTER 10

Kendra expertly maneuvered the small boat around obstructions and islands that were once the tops of mountains. Gatún Lake curved as it narrowed through Soberania National Park on one side and the protected Arraiján Forest on the other.

"Commander, I suggest we pull off the river under the Puente Centenario bridge and find a way up on top to take your pictures. On that side of the canal, there are three sets of old locks; the single lane Pedro Miguel, which is only one lock that feeds into Miraflores Lake. But the Miraflores locks have two lanes that empty into the Pacific Ocean. Then there are the new locks, the Cocoli, that are off to the right with one lane and three locks. From the bridge, though, you should have a good view of everything. The concrete sides are tall enough to keep you hidden."

"Sounds like a plan." Although Andrew had been through the Pacific locks several times, he didn't know them nearly as well as the Caribbean side. Before he could say anything else, his cell phone rang. "Buchanan."

"Dude…" It was Grant. "Where the hell are you?"

"On a mission for Charley." She had recently pulled Grant's ass out of a seriously bad situation, so he was familiar with the mysterious woman. Andrew wasn't sure how much more he was allowed to tell his friend so the less he said, the better at this point.

"Right. Okay. Charley. Of course." Grant gave a wry chuckle. "Have you've spoken to Ryker?"

"Uh, no. Why? What's going on?" He'd been avoiding Ryker and Ajax, the founders of the Holt Agency. He hadn't made his decision what he was going to do after he finished this cruise contract.

"I'm not in a position to say." That was SEAL speak for whatever he was doing was top secret and too many ears were around him.

"So, you've talked to Ryker. Did he receive a mission and assign it to you?"

"Yep."

"And I take it your mission is on board the cruise ship and you need my help." It figured; the minute he left, someone needed him.

"Absolutely. Please tell the captain to help us out." That didn't take as long as it could have. Sometimes one-way conversations were like the old *Password* game show.

"Hand this phone to Captain Phillips," Andrew ordered.

"Commander Buchanan, is that you?" Andrew recognized the captain's voice.

"Yes, sir. I don't know what the man, or men, in front of you need but I can tell you it's of vital importance to what we're all doing. Please give him whatever he asks for and it would probably be better for you if you didn't ask too many questions."

"There are several people here asking for the manifest." Andrew had no idea why Grant, and probably Holden, Tavis, and Keene would need the list of guests and their cabin numbers, but they obviously did. He would trust these men with his life, and by extension, trust the lives of all the guests on board.

"The men in front of you used to work for me," Andrew admitted, hoping the captain would read between the lines and understand that they too were SEALs.

"That's good enough for me. I'll give them anything they want."

"Thank you, sir. I'd appreciate it if you would hand the phone back to my friend."

"Andrew, thanks, pal." Grant was back on the line. "We've gotta run."

The line went dead.

What the hell happened to politeness? Even in the military people would say *thanks, bye.*

He slid his phone back into his pocket.

"I'm very worried," Nigel admitted. "Many people live in that area between the bridge and Panama City. Rich people. Very powerful."

"That's why we're here." Andrew put his hand on Nigel's shoulder and gave it a squeeze. "We need to find out exactly what the Chinese are up to. Were their orders to do nothing more than close the Panama Canal? Or take over its operations?" The latter didn't seem probable. By sinking ships in the canal, it could take months, maybe even years, to clear the lanes once again.

On the other hand, no military strategist would sink those ships without a way to raise them once they'd taken control. Was their goal to shut U.S. travel through the Panama Canal?

Or just stop the fleet strike force in the Caribbean from passing through?

"Which side of the river would you suggest?" Kendra took another bend in the river at full speed.

"The protected forest goes for several miles on the right, as does the raised portion of the bridge." Nigel pulled up a picture from the internet on his phone. "The mountains are steeper on the left, and there are more homes so there are more roads."

"It looks like there's some kind of industrial area just before and underneath the bridge." Andrew pointed to it on Nigel's phone. "Do you think we can tie up someplace along there? That looks like concrete."

"Yes, it is. They staged equipment there while building the bridge," Nigel explained.

Andrew started looking at the distance from the edge of the canal to roads that wound their way onto the bridge. That way would take too long. Hiking straight up the mountain through the woods was a mile at least. Not a trek he was looking forward to.

Kendra kept it very close to the side where she could be hidden under trees. As they approached the bridge support, they saw several boys fishing.

Nigel smiled. "Transportation." He climbed through the open hatch speaking Spanish. He and Andrew threw lines out to the boys who found places to securely tie the boat before they jumped down to the concrete abutment. Nigel spoke to the boys continually. They didn't look as young as Andrew had originally thought when they approached them.

Switching to English, Nigel translated, "They won't lend us their motor scooters, but they will take us up on top of the bridge...for a price."

Andrew shoved his hand into his pockets,

hoping he had more than a condom in his wallet. Since he rarely left the ship, he had no use for cash. "How much do they want?"

Several words were exchanged in Spanish before Nigel grinned. "They want your binoculars."

Damn. These were Andrew's personal binoculars. He'd had them for years, using them during his whole career in the Navy. Not only had they been expensive, but they also had sentimental value to him.

"Hold on." He quickly re-boarded the lifeboat and started digging through the cabinets.

"Bingo."

The lifeboat carried several sets of binoculars. They weren't as high quality as his, but he could offer them to the young men. As he dropped back down to the concrete, hands filled with binoculars, he scanned across the huge smiles of all the young men. "Ask them which one has the fastest scooter."

Thirty seconds later, they all pointed to the red scooters and the boys standing beside them. Andrew looked at Nigel, handing him one set of the binoculars. "Come on. You're going to be my translator."

All the boys followed, looking like a miniature version of a motorcycle gang. The road wound up the hill and looped around several times before they were on what looked like a divided interstate. They crossed over the canal and circled back around to be on the nearest side to the locks. In the middle of the bridge, they all stopped, lining the edge, peering through their new binoculars.

"Ask them if they saw what happened." Andrew needed to get as many details as possible.

Nigel listened to the young men for several minutes before interpreting. "They'd been fishing for about half an hour when the tanker went by. It cleared the first lock at Pedro Miguel and was in the second Miraflores lock when the explosion went off. Big black smoke came out of the ship. Within a few minutes, gunshots sounded but the young men couldn't see anything because of the black smoke. When it started to clear, the soldiers were lining each side of the locks. They've been trying to figure out what kind of soldiers they were because they didn't look like the normal Panamanian National Guard."

Andrew could easily see that the Chinese soldiers now controlled both the Miraflores and the Cocoli locks, but there was no ship blocking the new side. All the ships in Lake Gatún could get out—even their cruise ship—if the Chinese would let them through.

Taking out his satellite phone, he dialed Charley. As the phone rang, he carefully searched the hillside for a reconnaissance platoon or any sign of Chinese soldiers spreading out.

"Give me details," Charley demanded.

As quickly as possible he described everything he saw and promised pictures as soon as he hung up. "It looks to me as though their primary target was to close the Panama Canal." Andrew shook his head. "And they did a damn good job of it. But what I don't understand is why."

"Langley analysts believe it's to focus the world's attention on the canal and to force the fleet strike force to travel all the way around South America. That will give the Chinese an extra ten days to two weeks to take Taiwan before the American fleet can arrive and defend it." Charley's explanation made sense to the former Navy officer in him.

"Ma'am, what would you like me to do?" Other than report what he saw, he couldn't be much use to her.

Charley was quiet for a full minute. He thought he lost the connection when she finally spoke. "So, what you're telling me is that other than soldiers standing guard at the Cocoli locks, there's nothing blocking that exit."

"That's correct."

"Excellent," she said just above a whisper. "How many Chinese soldiers in total at the Pacific locks?"

Andrew had already counted. "Fifty-two, each armed with automatic machine guns carrying two extra magazines."

He heard talking in the background before she spoke clearly. "Commander, I want you to go back to Lake Gatún. Your boat is needed for a different mission. We have another mission for you. As soon as you're back on the cruise ship, I'll have more details." As usual, the line was dead.

"Tell them we need to get back to the boat." Andrew threw his leg over a red scooter and waited for its owner.

Nigel yelled and all the young men ran to their motorbikes.

As soon as the lifeboat was on its way back to the cruise ship, Andrew relayed the rest of the message to Kendra and Nigel.

"Do you think the United States is going to send in military?" Nigel's enthusiasm could barely be contained.

"I don't know." Andrew shrugged. To his surprise, his cell phone rang. "Buchanan."

"Chinese soldiers are boarding the cruise ship."

Andrew put the phone on speaker. "Say it again."

She repeated her exact words before continuing. "If chatter is to be believed, all they want are the cell phones. Seems the guests on board your ship were able to take photos and videos of the attack at Agua Clara locks. Your guests immediately posted them on all social media, and they went viral. As you know, all media in China is controlled by the government and they're not happy that the way they shut down the Panama Canal is on worldwide media. Videos of armed Chinese soldiers boarding your cruise ship are going up faster than they can round up the people."

Charley giggled. "I can't wait to see how they try to talk their way out of this one. Taking over the canal was one thing. Taking thousands of Americans hostage is a declaration of war against the United States. Now, I don't want you to panic. You know who's on board. As soon as they accomplish their first mission, they'll retake the ship. But they need your tender to finish the first mission, so I hope you're speeding your way back."

"Yes, ma'am," both he and Kendra said at the same time.

"It's still going to take another twenty-five minutes." Kendra had the throttles all the way down as the engines screamed around another bend.

"The aircraft carrier is turning into the wind and will launch reconnaissance aircraft as soon as it can. They don't want to launch helicopters until they have clear pictures of the area. Did you see any surface to air missiles?"

"No, ma'am. But they're damn big cargo carriers. No telling what's in any of those containers." Andrew refused to even venture a guess.

"Agreed. And any manifest would be bogus so no need to waste our time and efforts there. Captain Benson, get that boat back to your ship as fast as you can."

And the line went dead.

Andrew sent up a prayer for the four men who had been through so much already. Two missions. One on top of the other, and he was miles away, once again unable to help them. The feeling of déjà vu was strong. He prayed for a better ending than Holden, Tavis, and Keene had in Ethiopia. Grant didn't have it much better.

Kendra patted his arm. "They'll be fine. You trained them. I'm sure this isn't the first time they'd been on a mission that was compounded by the enemy."

She was right. He could do nothing about it until he got there. Worrying helped no one.

Andrew couldn't help himself; he bent down and gave her a kiss on the cheek. On the way past her ear, he whispered, "More where that's from when this shit's done."

She glanced quickly over her shoulder and smiled. "I'm going to hold you to that, sailor. I've been thinking, why would they only shut down three of the four exits? If their plan was to shut down the Panama Canal, any military strategist would shut down all four ways out."

"Fuck. You're right." His brain had been working on so many other things it hadn't considered the Chinese's strategy. "From what I've studied, the Chinese backup plans have backup plans."

"That means there's another ship out there with more Chinese soldiers and bombs." Kendra didn't look at him as she maneuvered her way through a narrow passage.

The satellite phone was in his hand and the buttons already pushed. He quickly relayed Kendra's thoughts, giving her complete credit.

"Somebody in this room thought about that too. Make a trip around the lake taking pictures of every ship. We'll cross-reference them. Wasn't the gate at Cocoli having problems this morning?"

"Yes, ma'am. That's what we were told." Andrew started to pace inside the small boat.

"Somebody find me the queue order for Cocoli this—" She'd hung up yelling at someone else in the room.

Andrew gave Kendra a huge hug and a smacking kiss. "You're a genius."

"I wouldn't go that far." Glancing over her shoulder, she smiled. "But thanks for the recognition."

"It was your idea." What the hell had she expected?

They could finally see the big white cruise ship anchored well offshore. Andrew let out the breath he was holding and quickly sucked in another as he realized what they might face when they reached the platform. First, though, they had to circle the lake taking pictures of every ship.

His cell phone rang.

This time he looked at the phone number. Charley.

"I'm sending a helicopter from the fleet in the Caribbean your way. They're going to land two miles away from the locks. Once they complete their first mission, they will be back to pick you up. I want you to give your report directly to the admiral on the aircraft carrier."

In true Charley manner, the line went dead.

Andrew relayed the information to Nigel and Kendra. He then decided to call Grant and get an update.

"Housman here." Grant spoke in a normal voice, not a whisper, so that was a good sign.

"Hey. On our way back." He didn't want to say too much. "Have you accomplished your first mission and retaken the ship?"

"Of course. Can we get out of here?" Leave it to his men to carry out both missions and face the next challenge.

"The old locks on the other side are toast, but the good news is the new locks are still open, at least for now. Well, except for the fifty armed Chinese soldiers. We believe that the ship that was supposed to blow those new locks is some-where on Lake Gatun. Charley is trying to identify it now. It's going to take some time. Then they're going to have to disarm it somehow before letting it go through the locks. And that would be after someone eliminates those fifty Chinese soldiers."

"Looks like we aren't going anywhere for a while then." Grant's voice sounded resigned.

"Even if the Panamanians get rid of the Chinese soldiers immediately, they'll refuse to let anyone into that lock until they find the fourth Chinese ship. They can't take a chance on it being successful. There's going to be a huge backlog of course. When they reopen those locks, they'll no doubt only be permitting one ship through at a time."

"Makes sense. I'm sure it's not safe to let people get off this ship in Panama. Too much unrest, but I'm with Justice Williams now. We need to get her safely transported back to the States."

"As in Supreme Court Justice Williams?"

"Yes." These men had accomplished more than he'd thought.

"I'll bet that's what the helicopters are for," Andrew said out loud. "Are you staying with her and her family once we get them off the ship?"

"No. Caroline will be with them. I'll start sweeping the ship to make sure no soldiers were left behind and keep an eye on any incoming boats." Grant was all business.

"Good. Thank God you guys were on this cruise. I can't imagine what would have happened without you." Andrew didn't want to give that scenario a single thought.

Grant chuckled. "I'm going to need a vacation after this vacation."

"Hang on a second," Andrew stated before the phone was muted. He used the satellite phone to confirm with Charley that the first wave of helicopters was to evacuate Justice Williams.

"I'm back," Andrew said. "Just confirmed there is a helicopter en route to pick up the justice and I understand she's traveling with her husband. When I arrive, we'll move the two of them to this lifeboat and transport them to the other side of the lake. ETA twenty minutes. Can you meet us on deck four starboard stern?"

"Yes. We'll be there."

"Have them take only what's mandatory. We'll pack up their room and ship their luggage to them as soon as it's possible."

"Got it. See you in twenty."

CHAPTER 11

KENDRA REDUCED THE SPEED OF THE BOAT AS SHE circled the lake so Andrew could take pictures of all the ships while Nigel continued to point out several hazards that were close to the surface. There were seven container ships—carrying multicolored boxes stacked high atop each other and as wide as the ship itself—similar to the ones blocking the three canals. Eleven were bulk carriers with sealed internal chambers for everything from grains to oil, and three reefer ships with refrigerated hulls to help keep their produce fresh.

The ships were flying flags from all over the world. After two decades at sea, Kendra knew that in today's global economy, where the ship was technically registered meant nothing.

At the Academy she'd learned that during World War II when even merchant vessels were being sunk, ship owners found it convenient to register in neutral countries. The practice continued during the Cold War when even the United States of America used Liberia's registry to build a fleet of neutral ships. Today, Panama had the largest registry in the world followed by Liberia, the Marshall Islands, Hong Kong, and Singapore. Nearly all the world's fleet was registered under a flag of a country other than its own.

Kendra always thought it was a crazy way to do business but understood the high taxes most first world countries put on maritime vessels, not to mention the marine regulations imposed by their own countries. Monarch Cruise Lines flew the flag of the Marshall Islands, so its owners paid no income tax and very little corporation tax. She supposed if she owned multiple cruise lines like their parent company, she'd do the same thing. In her job as staff captain, she was privy to the costs of how expensive it was to run just one ship.

Andrew double tapped the covered bow before he slid in through the hatch and immediately started uploading the pictures.

"Any idea which one it might be?" She turned the boat toward their own ship.

"There are two container ships that are flying the Chinese flag," he said without looking up from his phone, thumbs punching away.

As she neared her ship, she checked her phone. As soon as she was within Wi-Fi range, she called the bridge. "Have Ensign Dudley report to the lifeboat platform."

"What are you doing?" Andrew asked.

"I'm going wherever you go. Ensign Dudley can transport the Supreme Court justice to the waiting helicopters." She'd given this some serious thought. "If you're going to talk to someone in the fleet strike force, I might be able to help. Not only did I go to school with many of the senior officers, I probably know several of them personally."

Although she didn't keep up with her Naval Academy classmates as well as she should, most would recognize her. She'd broken a glass ceiling or two as she rose through the ranks. Her divorce had also caused waves throughout the dual officer family community.

She had heard that her guardian angel had pinned on his third star. If only she could be so lucky as to have Admiral Thurman at the helm of the fleet strike force in the Caribbean. Unfortunately, those were usually commanded by a rear admiral.

She maneuvered the lifeboat against the platform and the deck hands grabbed the lines thrown to them by Andrew and Nigel. Ensign Dudley climbed aboard. "Morning, ma'am.

Thank you for requesting me." The young woman's smile was sincere.

Kendra understood exactly how she felt. "Are you alright?"

"A little shaken but I can handle this boat. I love the feel of having a wheel in my hands. They...the soldiers...they made it to the bridge, but Captain Phillips stayed cool. He did what they asked and made the announcements." She sat down next to Kendra on the pilot bench. "It wasn't very long before men who were on the bridge earlier came back and took out the soldiers." Moving her body as though she were fighting, she explained, "They were fast. They'd taken the guns away from them so fast it was a blur."

Kendra smiled and leaned in. "I'm going to tell you a secret. They were Navy SEALs."

The ensign's eyes went wide then her grin became fiendish. "I wonder if any of them are single. I think we're going to be stuck here for a while so I'm not going to have many duties on the bridge."

They both laughed. "If you're serious, I'll find out." She glanced toward Andrew who was still on the phone. "I have connections."

"Yes, please." Her request was quiet as she nodded.

"Let's go," Andrew said as he passed by her.

She followed him through the hatch onto the

platform, offering her hand down. He immediately went over and shook his friend's hand. If she remembered right, he was Grant.

"Thank you." Andrew sounded truly grateful. "Can you please escort them to the helicopter?" He nodded toward the mid-fifties couple nervously standing next to Grant's girlfriend. She'd forgotten her name. Callie? Maybe. "I'll feel better if you're with them. Plus, you're armed and trained in case anything goes wrong."

"Of course."

"Ready when you are, sir." Ensign Dudley peered through the lifeboat hatch.

Andrew turned and pointed to the three waiting guests. "You take them and bring Grant and Callie back."

"Yes, sir." She saluted even though he wasn't in his official uniform.

Callie pulled her phone out of her pocket and took a step away, pressing the phone to her ear and covering the other to hear over the roar of the idling lifeboat. She nodded as she listened and then ended the call. "I need to go with them."

"Do you mean in the helicopter?" Andrew clarified.

"Yes." But Callie was looking at Grant, not Andrew.

Grant nodded. "Let's go."

The ensign assisted Justice Williams and her

husband into the lifeboat first before Callie. Grant was the last to board.

"You are required to wear life vests—" Ensign Dudley instructed as she closed the hatch.

Kendra watched them pull away then followed Andrew up to the bridge. He made a phone call on his way up and was met by his second-in-charge when he entered the door.

"Sir, I need you to officially put Sergeant Avadhut in charge of security until I return. Although he's not an officer, he's been my second-in-command for the past three months and I can vouch for his capability," Andrew told Captain Phillips.

Kendra hadn't expected that but completely understood why Andrew had done it. Somebody needed to be in charge of security while he was off the ship. Hopefully their trip to meet with the admiral of the fleet wouldn't take long.

"So be it." Captain Phillips nodded toward the new security officer. "I'm sorry to say this doesn't come with a pay raise or any official promotion, but it does need to be noted in the log." He said the latter looking at her.

Kendra immediately went to a computer, opened the official log, and made note. She also wrote that she and Andrew had left the ship and were leaving again with a very brief explanation as to why and where they were going.

While she'd been typing, Andrew had been

explaining the lock situation and how he and Kendra would be going to the aircraft carrier via helicopter that was going to land on the chopper pad.

"I'll go clear it now," Avadhut said as he left the bridge.

"I have no idea how long it will take to open the Agua Clara locks so this ship can return to the Caribbean." Andrew continued briefing Captain Phillips. "As I said, there is a possibility that the Chinese will allow all the ships in Lake Gatún to exit through the Cocoli locks into the Pacific."

"I'll contact headquarters with an update." The captain strode to the emergency phone line. "Since we're on the leading edge of information, and they're required by law to work through political channels, it's going to be quite a while before they give us direction."

"Hopefully I'll know a lot more by the time we get back." She didn't want to give him false hope but there were certain scenarios that would allow them to leave Lake Gatún sooner rather than later. "We need to continue positive communication with our guests."

As she said that, Kendra realized that fell under her responsibility. "I'll call an emergency staff meeting right now."

Captain Phillips reached for the microphone used to make ship wide announcements.

"Good afternoon, ladies and gentlemen. This is Captain Phillips speaking to you from the bridge. I, for one, would like to thank the very brave former U.S. Navy SEALs for recapturing our ship. We were so fortunate that they were on board sailing with us. Can I hear a round of applause for our four saviors?"

Cheering and clapping could be heard all over the ship.

"I regret to announce that due to the disturbance in the Agua Clara locks that we left this morning, all excursions into Panama have been canceled. Monarch Cruise Lines will reimburse you for those excursions. Until we hear from the Panamanian government when we can exit through the locks, we're going to remain anchored here. I promise I will keep you apprised of any updates. In the meantime, I encourage you to take advantage of all our ship's entertainment. Thank you."

By the time his announcement was finished, Kendra had every department officer in their boardroom. "First, I want to thank each and every one of you for the wonderful job that you did when the Chinese soldiers boarded the ship." She glanced over at Andrew. "See, all those first-person shooter drills paid off."

There were mumbles of agreement and thanks as they nodded toward Andrew.

"As I'm sure you've already heard the rumor, I

will confirm that Agua Clara is blocked and currently held by Chinese soldiers. No, I don't know why they did that or how long it will last. That's for the politicians to determine. But what we need to do now is to keep all our guests calm and entertained. It's going to be a while before we're able to leave Lake Gatún."

"Exactly how long is a while?" The commander of food and beverage asked the million-dollar question.

"I have no idea." That was an honest answer. "Prepare for a week." She knew they had food and water on board for at least that long since they weren't slated to return to their U.S. port for seven more days. She'd have to figure out the logistics of resupplying the ship after that amount of time.

She focused her attention on the entertainment director. "You are going to have the biggest job immediately. Because we don't know the political climate between China and Panama, Commander Buchanan has determined it's not safe for our guests to take their planned excursions into Panama."

"Makes sense," the lieutenant junior grade agreed. "I'll talk to the theater cast and get them working up something they can do around the pool tomorrow. We can add some bingo games and—"

"I don't have time for details. Just make it

happen." She scanned her senior officers' faces. "The most important thing we can do right now is keep our guests calm and informed. Now, I know the staff are the biggest gossips, so I want you to control the information. The captain will be making announcements as he receives them. Use sentences such as 'We don't know that for sure and by you saying that, that's how dangerous rumors get started.' And 'stick to the facts.' Check your manuals and use some of the corporate suggestions."

Kendra glanced toward Andrew who stepped to the front of the crowded room. "Captain Benson and I will be picked up shortly by a U.S. Navy helicopter. A carrier strike force was supposed to go through the entire canal starting this evening so it's only a few hundred miles out in the Caribbean. She and I are former Navy officers and have been asked to attend a briefing on board the aircraft carrier. When we return, we'll hopefully have good news."

Andrew stepped back, so Kendra continued, "Your number one job is to keep our guests calm and entertained. Make good decisions." With that she turned her back on them as an indication of dismissal.

She and Andrew walked side-by-side to their cabins. For the first time in weeks, they didn't sneak a kiss or a tender touch. It was as though they'd both shifted into command mode.

Not knowing when she'd be able to use the bathroom again, she quickly did so. Washing her hands, she took a good look at herself in the mirror. Not bad for almost forty-one years old. She quickly ran a brush through her hair and tied it in a bun at the back of her neck like she'd worn it for ten years in the Navy. She swiped on mascara and lip gloss, her feminine armor, and decided she looked good enough to meet some of her former classmates or senior officers.

As she walked past her open jewelry box, her shiny new captain's eagles glinted in the light.

Oh, yeah.

She grabbed two and pinned them on the epaulets of her lightweight navy blue windbreaker. Every Navy ship she'd ever served on, the bridge had been cold enough to hang meat. She'd wear the jacket to cover up her pointing nipples, guaranteed to show through the lightweight white uniform blouse. At least, that was her story, and she was sticking to it.

At the knock on her door, she immediately opened it to Andrew.

"Chopper will be here in five."

She stepped through the door and shut it behind her. "I'm ready."

As they headed down two flights of stairs, Andrew's phone rang.

Charley, he mouthed as he stopped in the stairwell.

"Yes, ma'am." He then motioned for her to step beside him. He tilted the phone so she could hear.

"We've identified the ship containing explosives and about thirty men in the hold of the ship. You're going to take control of that ship. I'm sending you the coordinates now."

"How the hell am I going to do that?" She could tell the words just slipped out of Andrew's mouth.

"Your mission to see the admiral has changed. He's going to give you everything and anything you need." Charley paused for a long moment before she continued. "This isn't for public knowledge but there are fifty SEALs on board the carrier, over a thousand Marines distributed over several ships, and weapons to support all of them double and triple."

They'd been expecting trouble, if not on the way, certainly once they arrived in the China Sea.

"Ma'am, I want you to be very clear. Are you expecting me to command military troops?" Andrew slumped down on a step so Kendra sat down to join him and continue to listen. "I'm no longer a commissioned officer."

"Don't you worry about that. It's being handled." Charley's authoritative voice left no room to question.

"Yes, ma'am."

"Just figure out how many men and what

equipment you'll need to capture that ship tonight."

Tonight? How could he ever put together a team and execute the hastily made plan within just a few hours? Were they setting him up for failure? Kendra was worried that she was there as nothing more than a witness to her lover's failure.

"Yes, ma'am." Andrew's response was casual as though she'd asked him to do nothing out of the ordinary.

Maybe that was the way SEALs worked. She had no idea.

"And once we gain control of the ship, what do you want us to do with it?" Andrew asked Charley.

"Is Captain Benson listening to this conversation?"

Kendra stared at the phone. How did Charley know she was there? "Yes, ma'am. I'm here."

"Excellent. Captain Benson, you're going to drive that ship to Panama City where the Panamanian government will seize the ship and everything on board...including the explosives and soldiers. So, Commander Buchanan, don't kill the soldiers." There were multiple voices in the background. "Okay, don't kill *all* the soldiers. They will be the proof Panama needs to show the world that China attacked Panama and crippled world commerce."

"Yes, ma'am," she and Andrew said in unison.

"Commander Buchanan, do you have everything I asked you to bring?"

"Yes, ma'am."

"You'd better."

The line went dead.

CHAPTER 12

ANDREW FOLLOWED KENDRA TO THE HELICOPTER landing pad snuggled into the very bow of the ship. Unless looked at from the sky, the green decking looked like nothing more than an area painted for a game. Like so many other things aboard a cruise ship, it too had multiple purposes. Earlier that day had been crowded with guests trying to get the perfect picture of the locks. It had been completely emptied and swept clean of debris by the acting security officer.

"Ladies and gentlemen, this is Captain Phillips coming to you from the bridge. I ask that everyone stay away from the bow until the U.S. Navy helicopter lifts completely off the deck with Captain Kendra Benson and Commander Andrew Buchanan on board. They are both former U.S. Navy officers and have been invited to the fleet for briefing. Those ships are waiting in the Caribbean Sea to start transiting the entire Panama Canal this evening."

Andrew searched the skies and couldn't see or hear any incoming helicopter. He knew it would come. Charley never gave him bad intelligence.

The captain continued his spiel. "I have an interesting fact for you. Part of the reason the new locks were built, starting in 2007 and completed in 2016, was so the U.S. fleet could move more quickly from one ocean to the other. Their ships had grown considerably larger since the original locks were designed and built, finishing construction in 1914."

He heard it first, not one but several helicopters heading their way. They approached from all four directions. He shouldn't have been surprised that they sent four Seahawks armed with Hellfire missiles carrying machine guns or that the powerful birds circled the sky. A fifth Seahawk, without armament, seemed to drop straight out of the sky.

Captain Phillips's voice boomed over the speakers. "I want you to give Captain Benson and Commander Buchanan a rousing sendoff." Andrew could barely hear him over the noise of the turning rotors.

Never before had Andrew boarded a Navy aircraft with so much fanfare. As a SEAL, they often snuck out in the dark of night doing everything within their power to not gain a glance of attention.

Kendra stopped and waved, a huge smile pasted on her face. "Wave, damn it," she said through two rows of bright white teeth.

Andrew turned and waved briefly as the helicopter touched down, never slowing its blades. They were treating the ship as though it were a hot landing zone.

"Come on." He wanted to take Kendra's hand and run to the helicopter, but this was definitely not the time for PDA. Allowing her to step in first, he did admire that perfect ass of hers.

As soon as he sat down, a crewman handed him a helmet. He turned to instruct Kendra, but it was already properly on her head, and she was adjusting the microphone. Even through the helmet, he could hear the guests on board the ship cheering them on.

"You seem very much at home," Andrew told her once his communication system was connected.

"You forget, or maybe you didn't know, that I was commanding officer of a destroyer and they have two Seahawks on board. Out to sea, this was the only way to move to the carrier for meetings." Kendra looked over her shoulder and smiled at him. "Trust me, I had lots of practice strapping into a chopper."

"Ma'am, are you Commander Ward?" one of the pilots asked.

"I haven't been called that in ten years," she corrected him. "I'm Captain Benson."

"It's a pleasure to have you aboard, again." The helicopter lifted off and gently swooped along one side of the ship as it gained altitude. "I was with you in the Med. Sit back and relax, we'll be there in about ten minutes. We didn't see any hostiles on the way in but the admiral insisted on an armed escort."

Exactly as the pilot predicted, ten minutes later he set the big bird down as gently as a butterfly. The door slid open, and they were met by two commanders. After giving Kendra a hand down, the first one asked, "May I have your names, please?"

"Captain Kendra Benson, Monarch Cruise Lines." She took the lead and continued with the introductions. "This is our security officer, Commander Andrew Buchanan."

With nothing more than a nod the same man ordered, "Follow me."

Per Charley's instructions, Andrew slid in his Bluetooth ear buds and dialed the mysterious woman. He wasn't sure why she wanted to listen to their conversation, but Andrew never questioned her orders.

As they entered the gray-on-gray bridge, the

admiral faced forward with his back to them. They were underway so perhaps they had other aircraft out. Andrew always thought it was exciting to watch the jets land on the carrier deck. Perhaps they were waiting for the one now.

The air boss lowered his binoculars. "All little birds are in the nest. Recon is on standby."

"Sir, Captain Kendra Benson and Commander Andrew Buchanan from Monarch Cruise Lines are here to see you." At the names, the admiral cocked his head slightly to the side.

Like a king perched on his throne, the admiral slowly turned his chair around. Never giving Andrew even a glance, he stared at Kendra. "I see you've gone back to your maiden name. I'm sorry to hear that, sweetheart. I always thought Kendra Ward was a beautiful name."

Andrew glanced at Kendra just as her shoulders slumped a fraction before she squared them and straightened her back. "A lot has happened in ten years. I've certainly changed but I see you haven't improved one damn bit. You're still an arrogant, cocky bastard."

The admiral grinned. "You used to like my cock...and every senior officer you ever served under. You brought new meaning to that phrase."

"I didn't need to fuck my way up the chain of command; I was damn good at my job and you know it." She put on that shit-eating grin she wore when she knew she was right. "You couldn't stand the fact that a woman had higher review marks than you did. The fact that I was your wife pissed you off even more."

Every set of eyes on the bridge moved to stare at Kendra...including Andrew's.

Wife? He had no idea she'd even been married before. How had he missed that?

They'd never talked much about their time in the Navy or any of their past for that matter. There wasn't much he could say since most of his missions were top secret, need to know only.

He mentally shrugged. He'd never told Kendra about Abigail, his cheating fiancée. But a three-month foiled engagement didn't compare to a marriage.

Kendra's gaze swept the deck. "I see you haven't changed in the last ten years. You're still the misogynistic asshole you were back then. There doesn't seem to be a single woman on this bridge."

"I'd plant a woman right here next to me if I could find one qualified." Nodding at all the men surrounding him, expecting agreement, he sat back on his throne.

Andrew noticed that most of the men quickly shifted their eyes forward. No one was going to disagree with the most senior officer, but that didn't mean they had to agree with him. Andrew had played that game himself a time or two, looking away so his personal thoughts couldn't be seen on his face.

"Women have been on warships since 1994," Kendra pointed out. "Don't you think it's time you stepped into the twenty-first century?"

"I see you finally made captain." The abrupt change in subject jolted Andrew almost as much as the admiral's backhanded comment to Kendra.

She smiled at her ex-husband. "Yes. You know, we command very similar ships. Like you, I oversee a city at sea with over five thousand souls."

"We may have the same number of people on board, but you don't have airplanes and heli-copters...or guns."

Andrew had had enough. He was over this pompous ass demeaning Kendra every chance he got. "Speaking of guns and weapons, I think we need to refocus on why we're here."

Every man on the bridge glanced toward Andrew before returning their gaze to their work. "Thank you for the live afternoon soap opera but I'm pretty sure every officer on this bridge has heard you badger your ex-wife enough. I know I have." He stepped next to Kendra. "We have been given orders from high in the government to report our findings to you. And then you are supposed to provide me with whatever I'm going to need to capture the fourth Chinese ship that's still carrying bombs and soldiers."

"About fucking time," Charley congratulated him in his ear where only he could hear. "Ward is such a fucking asshole. Let's see if he gives you any grief."

Admiral Ward crossed his arms over his chest, just above his growing belly, and leaned back in his seat with a sneer. "I'm not sure what else you can tell me that I don't already know. Three Chinese container ships have sunk in the canal, blocking our way through it. Chinese soldiers are lining both sides of the canal. There is no sign of Panamanian canal operators, so I have no idea if they're being held hostage, or they've killed them."

Andrew jumped in as the admiral took a breath. "They killed them. The soldiers shot them and threw their bodies into the canal where they were eaten by the crocodiles."

"Gruesome but effective." The information didn't seem to faze the admiral. "What other important details do you have to tell me?"

"The Chinese soldiers haven't moved beyond the canal, not even a reconnaissance team." Andrew decided to give the brash man only facts. "The fourth ship that was supposed to be in the Cocoli locks at the same time as the others is still floating in Lake Gatún. My orders are that you are to give me whatever I need to secure that ship. What I need is fifteen to twenty of the SEALs you're carrying."

"What makes you think I'm carrying SEALs?" Admiral Ward cocked his head to the side and stared at Andrew as if daring him to answer.

"As I said, our orders come from high in the government." He wasn't going to tell him about Charley. Hell, he didn't know enough about the woman to tell him anything vital.

"And why the fuck would I allow you to take command of these SEALs I supposedly have on board?" The admiral leaned forward, looking down at Andrew. "And if I did have them, I would order my men to take over the Chinese ship if in fact they are on board the ship; they're in my fleet thus under my command. I can't turn over active-duty seamen just because you come in here asking for them. What makes you think you could handle a platoon of SEALs?"

"Don't worry about this posturing asshole," Charley ordered. "You're getting everything you need. The admiral's phone is going to ring in a minute. Make sure he answers it personally."

"Because I have been on more dangerous operations than this one." Andrew wondered how fast Admiral Ward would find out that he'd been court-martialed and removed from the Navy.

A phone rang. Every bridge officer scanned to

see which one it was. Dubbed the bat phone—because when it rang, somebody in Washington wanted to speak directly to whoever was in charge—the phone rang again.

"Admiral, you need to answer that." Andrew was proud he held in his smug tone.

The senior officer looked at him as though Andrew had just asked him to mop the floor. He acted as though it was beneath him to answer a telephone.

"Tell him the chief of naval operations wants to talk to him," Charley said.

Andrew held in the chuckle and grin. "Sir, the chief of naval operations wants to speak with you...on that phone." He pointed to the red phone with the red blinking light.

Blazing eyes shot daggers at him. "How the fuck do you know that?" Without looking away, he bellowed, "Officer of the day, answer the fucking phone."

A lieutenant wearing a white helmet and white belt, fully armed, ran forward and plucked the old-fashioned phone out of its cradle. Ten seconds later, he handed the phone to the admiral. "Admiral Ward, the chief of naval operations wishes to speak to you."

Saying not a word, the admiral held out his hand. The lieutenant placed the hand piece in the admiral's palm then quickly retreated.

"Admiral Ward," he announced.

Charley began a running commentary of the CNO's half of the conversation. "He's being told to give you any support that you want. He is to give you as many of the SEAL team that you're requesting. He's depicted best platoon and will be prepared to back you up in any way you need."

"Why would I give him sixteen more men to kill?" Admiral Ward snapped.

Oh, fuck. He knows who I am, and he knows about—

"Andrew." Charley's voice brought him back to her, cutting off any attempt for him go down that dark hole. "The CNO is telling him that you didn't kill anyone. He's explaining to him that those men survived and are happily retired civilians. He's also telling them that three of the survivors are currently on board your cruise ship."

There was a moment of silence before she spoke again. "He just told the admiral that you were the scapegoat and that you weren't responsible for those orders...Admiral Ward was. Technically, he was Captain Ward at the time."

Charley giggled and Andrew's eyes grew wide. He'd never heard her giggle or do anything else feminine. "The CNO just told the pretentious ass in front of you that he'd better make you happy because if you talked, Admiral Ward might end up in Fort Leavenworth military prison."

"Yes, sir." The admiral hung up the phone and

stared at it for a long moment. "Send for Commander Crockett."

Andrew couldn't be that lucky. Had "Davy" been promoted to commander? Was he the CO of the SEALs on board?

When the admiral finally raised his head and looked at Andrew, defeat painted every age wrinkle on his face a shade of gray. The man suddenly looked twenty years older. "You have my full cooperation." Gone was the arrogant tone and self-righteous demeanor. In his place was a chastened man.

Moments later a familiar face entered the bridge. Scott "Davy" Crockett strode in with the swagger only a SEAL could back up. "As I live and breathe, Andrew Buchanan." The man opened his arms wide and pulled him into a back-thumping hug. Andrew was so shocked he didn't respond for at least a full second.

Although he and Scott were in different BUD/S classes, they knew each other well. The SEAL community was very small, especially among the officers. After the Ethiopian debacle, Andrew didn't know if any SEAL officer would even speak to him, even though he'd been exonerated. All that had happened after he'd left the Navy.

"You got fucking shafted," his friend whispered as he pounded Andrew's back. "Talk more in private." As they separated, Davy smiled and said loudly, "I've been given orders to provide you with a platoon. Come down to my office and we'll look at personnel records. I'd like to bounce a few ideas around with you for our other missions since you've had eyes on the targets."

"Commander Crockett, you have the full cooperation of this fleet." The admiral stepped down off his high chair and approached the two SEALs. Speaking in low tones, he warned, "We don't have permission from the Panamanian government to capture the locks. We do, though, have the go-ahead to capture the Chinese vessel. I'd rather you plan both missions at the same time, so we have the absolute element of surprise."

"Absolutely," both commanders said at the same time.

"We have eyes in the sky. Satellite photos and fresh pictures are coming in constantly from reconnaissance planes." At the admiral's direction, they stepped off the bridge. "I just authorized both of you access to the CIC. I want to see any plans you have the minute you decide. We might not have time to run things up the ladder. Come straight to me."

Kendra stepped out into the hall. "You didn't think you were going to do this without me, did you?"

"Of course not." Andrew looked directly into Admiral Ward's eyes. "You've cleared Captain Benson for the Command Information Center as well, right?"

The admiral stared silently down at his ex-wife for a long moment.

Andrew wasn't about to back down. "She was with me as we reconned all four locks. She has her own observations."

"Yes. I suppose she needs to be in there, too." He turned to reenter the bridge. "She'll have permission by the time you get there."

As soon as the door closed, Andrew introduced Kendra to Scott Crockett.

"Call me Davy. No one calls me Scott except my wife and mother." He held the door open to the CIC. "Besides, no one here will know who you're talking to." He shifted his gaze to Andrew. "Do you still go by Zed?"

"Not since I left the Navy." Andrew didn't know how he felt about using his handle once again. In ways, it felt right. Once again, he was completely surrounded by everything U.S. Navy. Ships had a certain smell that almost felt like home. The lingo in the Navy was so different from that on a cruise ship. He understood the necessity of handles and nicknames while on a mission. "It's probably a good idea to call me Zed."

Davy slapped him on the shoulder. "Like old times, huh."

"I don't have a handle," Kendra said as she stepped into the darkened room. "Do I get to pick my own?"

"Hell, no." Davy grinned over his shoulder at her. "We'll find you one."

CHAPTER 13

ANDREW WAS PULLED ASIDE BY DAVY AS SOON AS they walked into the CIC, leaving Kendra to walk around and gaze at the backlit pictures circling the room of the locks and the Lake Gatún.

"Hey, man, I want to tell you how sorry I am about the way the court-martial turned out." Davy dropped his head and looked at his boots. Returning his gaze to Andrew, he confessed, "I knew by the looks on their faces the minute I started to tell them what an awesome SEAL and outstanding commanding officer you were that they'd already judged you guilty. If even half the rumors I've heard are true, you were nothing but a scapegoat."

What could he say? "They had to hang somebody out to dry. I was the last one to issue the orders. I didn't push hard enough to find bodies." The last part was what hurt the most. There should have been more left to identify. When the search team hadn't found anything, it should have rung alarm bells. But local CIA informants swore all the SEALs had been blown up in the explosion and the brass chose to believe them.

Davy grabbed his shoulder and squeezed. "Are you doing okay? I heard they gave you nothing but the duffel bag you came in with."

Andrew clutched his elbow and squeezed back, touched by the other man's concern. "I'm doing fine. I don't know if you've heard but the truth is all the men in that platoon are alive and home. They'd been captured by Ethiopian rebels and treated as prisoners of war. Some were hurt pretty bad, but they all got out of that godforsaken country alive. I wish I could say I had something to do with it, but I can't. I was sequestered to my quarters by then with zero contact with anyone except my attorney. Then, as you well know, court-martialed for their deaths."

He shrugged before he continued, "After all the men were returned home, they couldn't very well say *oops, we made a mistake*. I guess they did what they could for all of us. I'm technically retired as a lieutenant commander, which, by the way, doesn't pay shit. I have a guardian angel, though, who actually found out the men were captive rather than dead. She sent the two SEALs who were left for dead at the explosion site back in to rescue them. It gets really dirty from there."

Andrew scanned the room and found Kendra standing close to a picture of the Cocoli locks. He returned his attention to Davy. "This goes no further than you, but somehow the vice president's son and ambassador to Ethiopia's stepson were involved." Andrew gave the man a sarcastic grin. "As you can see, the cover-up was deep."

"H-o-l-y fuck." Davy drew out the first word. "It's no wonder you get anything that you want with this mission."

Andrew shrugged again. "I don't know if that's it or if it's just another way to keep their noses clean. 'Former SEAL Goes Rogue' will be the title of the report if it all goes to shit."

Davy smacked him on the back. "Let's go plan a mission that doesn't go to shit."

The two men turned and joined Kendra.

"Find anything new or different?" Andrew asked.

"Yeah, this looks like a changing of the guard." She pointed to the ship in the Cocoli lock. "It looks as though these men are coming from the ship." She moved down a few pictures. "And here it looks as though they are replacing the men standing sentinel along the sides."

"Good catch." Davy pointed to the timestamp. "Let's check the next pass. We might want to find the changing of the guard so that we get them all while they're outside. Clearing a ship is a pain in the ass."

"Agreed. Were these taken from a surveillance plane or the satellite?" Andrew found the officer in charge of the CIC and got his answer. "Can you order another pass in say four hours and again in six?" He brought the man over to the picture and pointed out their findings.

"Sure." The man left, returning a few minutes later. "Done. What else you need? I've been given orders for complete cooperation."

"Can you pull up a tabletop map of Lake Gatún?" Kendra asked. "That way we can all look at it up close."

"Certainly." He led them over to a large table near the center of the room then ordered a projection of the lake.

"There are about fifty Chinese soldiers holding each of the locks so that's a hundred and fifty," Andrew stated.

"We can then assume that there are another fifty on board the container ship in Lake Gatún." Kendra pointed to the ship in the middle of a lake.

"There may not be as many in the Cocoli locks because they're so close in proximity to the Miraflores." Davy circled the two sets of locks with his finger. "They're practically side-by-side. Versus the Agua Clara locks and the old Gatún locks that are nearly a mile apart separated by a hill covered in the dense trees."

"The Chinese don't do anything without

backup plans for their backup plans. I'll bet my next month's salary that the soldiers are eating and sleeping inside the ship." Kendra thought another moment. "I'd go as far as to say they had to have reconfigured one of the bulk storage rooms into barracks and possibly even a second kitchen to handle all the additional personnel. A normal carrier only has twenty to thirty crew aboard and three to four of them are cooks. To feed that many soldiers it would take two to three times as many support personnel. Then there's the heads. They would've had to add at least three more bathrooms with showers. It's a long way from China to Panama."

Andrew and Davy exchanged a glance. "Thirty days?"

Davy nodded. "We've been that long without showers."

Kendra scrunched her face. "Yuck!"

"You do what you gotta do," Andrew explained.

Shaking her head, Kendra suggested, "Let's move on."

"Yes, ma'am." Davy shifted his gaze to the photo on the wall. "If we can catch them during change of guard, we'll be able to take out more at one time." He raised one eyebrow. "Kill or capture?"

Andrew didn't see any other way to take the vessel or the locks without killing Chinese soldiers. "Capture creates a whole new set of problems, but I don't have final orders yet. For now, let's just plan on retaking the canal."

For the next fifteen minutes, they planned ways to insert SEALs to regain control of the canals. The CIC officer walked up and listened to their Plan A and Plan B. "Seems like a waste of SEALs to hold the locks especially when we have an entire Marine Expeditionary Unit deployed with us. Those guys are trained to hold an encampment."

Andrew, Kendra, and Davy glanced from one to another. "Well, damn. Sounds like a job for the Marines."

They then went about deciding how many Marines needed to be in place to hold the locks, how to insert them and rotate them out as necessary until an encampment could be established. A MEU always included an engineer support battalion, prepared to establish an entire base in the middle of nowhere. They, too, would need support in the form of everything from bathrooms to food.

Two hours later they had a workable plan. Several more times they had included the CIC officer to clarify available assets and offer his opinions and suggestions. Just as they were about to run through everything again, because twice was never enough, Admiral Ward walked in with the captain in charge of the air wing beside him.

"Please tell me you have a plan." The admiral stepped up to the back-lighted table and leaned over, looking at Lake Gatún.

"This has been a very cooperative effort. The CIC officers have been extremely helpful." Kendra took over as the senior officer of the group. "First, starting immediately, we would like helicopters and planes flying over Lake Gatún from all different directions at irregular intervals. We don't want them to know which direction an attack is coming from, or when. In a way, we want to desensitize them to air traffic."

"Done." Admiral Ward looked over his shoulder at the head of the air wing.

"You may want to ask the senior Marine of the MEU to join us," Andrew suggested.

"You're using Marines?" The admiral looked shocked.

"Yes, sir. As you will see as we go through the plan, they are integral in holding the locks and keeping the salvage team safe," Davy explained. "The SEALs will go in and take the locks, hopefully during change of guard when most of the Chinese soldiers are on the ground. We'll attack in three places at once to maintain the element of surprise." He pointed to the three locks. He didn't expound upon how they would take it or how many lives they would take in the process.

Davy continued, "This is where we need the Marines. They need to come in right behind us and hold the locks while we board the ships and clear them of all personnel."

The admiral nodded. "Good plan...so far. What about the ship in the middle of Lake Gatún?"

It was Andrew's turn to take over the briefing. "I'll take a fourth platoon and we'll jump onto the ship. It will be easier if we start from the top down since the ship is still under power. We'll take the bridge, leaving her with one of the Chinese-speaking SEALs and a guard, then clear our way down deck by deck. That should give Captain Benson time to sort out the bridge."

"What the hell do you mean, time for Kendra to sort out the bridge?" Admiral Ward stared at his ex-wife.

"First of all, that's none of your business." Kendra sounded a little snippy, but Andrew didn't blame her. "But as you are the admiral providing us with support, I'll share my mission with you. I have been ordered to take control of the Chinese container ship."

"No!" The admiral stood up straight and pounded his fist on the glass-topped table. "No way in hell am I going to let you board an enemy ship during a wartime situation." He stepped closer to her and held out his hand as though he was going to grab her arm but dropped it at the glare she gave him. "Sweetheart, I can't let you do that. I can't put you in harm's way. You...you might get hurt...or worse." He turned and walked back to his original position and punched his balled fists on his hips. "No. Absolutely not."

Kendra straightened her back and squared her shoulders. "First of all, you have no say in this matter. I am no longer in the U.S. Navy, and thank God, I am no longer your wife. I take my orders from a higher source."

Interrupting their showdown, the colonel in charge of the MEU strode up to the table. "I understand the Marines are needed."

"Yes, sir." Kendra ignored her ex-husband and proceeded to brief the newcomer. "We're using SEALs to take all three locks at the same time, but we need your Marines to come in right behind them. Plan on holding the locks until the salvage team can get the Chinese container ships out of the way. We plan to land everyone on the Caribbean side right here, the same place they evacuated the Supreme Court justice and her husband. It's an excellent landing site, two miles away from Agua Clara and the old Gatún locks. It's hidden from locks themselves."

The Marine colonel turned to the captain commanding the air wing. "I'll give you a list of what we need for transport within the hour. My men are spread over several ships so we will need to consolidate them here on the carrier starting immediately."

"Understood."

"What about the Pacific side?" the colonel asked.

"Landing everyone, SEALs first followed almost immediately by the Marines, at the U.S. Embassy. It has a landing pad behind high walls so no one can see who is coming and going." Kendra then looked at Admiral Ward. "You may want to check with the embassy to see if they need to be evacuated. The same helicopters that drop off the SEALs and the Marines can be used to remove the evacuees. That may involve more Marines, though, to assist in the evacuation."

The admiral nodded. "Since there will be fighting so close, I'm sure the ambassador and his family will want to be removed. We'll find quarters for them here until they can be shipped out with the Supreme Court justice and her family."

At the mention of a justice, the colonel swung his gaze to the admiral. "When did they arrive?"

"About six hours ago. They were aboard a cruise ship that is stuck in Lake Gatún." The admiral spoke without inflection.

"My cruise ship that was boarded by Chinese soldiers while we were out on a recon run," Kendra explained. "The four SEALs who were vacationing on my ship rescued the justice and her family."

"Glad they're safe." The colonel looked over the map. "What else do you need Marines for?"

Andrew spoke this time. "Until our mission changes, that's all, sir."

"Admiral, by your leave."

"Dismissed," he said with a nod.

Before the colonel was out of the room, Andrew's phone rang. One look at the caller ID and he wasn't sure if he was happy or not. "I have to take this. It's Charley."

"In the middle of a briefing you're going to take a phone call from some broad named Charley?" The admiral was back to his indignant self.

"Yes. She's my boss, for now." Into the phone he answered, "Andrew Buchanan."

"Where are you?"

Andrew was almost surprised that she didn't know his exact location. Charley always seemed to know everything.

"In the CIC with Admiral Ward, Captain Benson, Commander Crockett of the Navy SEALs on board, and the commanding officer of the strike force air contingent." Andrew suddenly realized he'd never gotten the captain's name. Oh, well. At this point it didn't matter.

"Put the phone on speaker. I want everybody to hear this."

"Yes, ma'am." Andrew laid the phone on the table after turning it on speaker and increasing the volume all the way to high.

"I'm not taking orders from anyone from a cruise line," Admiral Ward huffed.

"No, you're not. You're taking orders from the chief of naval operations who has already given you your orders, which are to support Commander Buchanan and Captain Benson." Charley sounded pissed.

"Who the hell are you to give me orders?"

Charley chuckled. "Someone who takes her orders directly from the president of the United States, your commander-in-chief. I'm currently standing in a war room in the Pentagon with the Joint Chiefs of Staff. Personally, if I were you, I would shut the fuck up and say nothing other than yes ma'am, yes sir."

At least Admiral Ward had the courtesy to apologize. "Forgive me, ma'am. Until your explanation I had no idea who you were." Under his breath he added, "I still don't but I'm listening."

"That's a good start." Deep voices could be heard in the background. "Andrew, Kendra, you are both now officially contracted to the Panamanian government and all actions from this point forward will be under their oversight. You will be paid by them through me. By the way, we're being paid very well. And Admiral Ward, even though this is above your pay grade, I'm going to let you in on a little piece of top-secret information. The U.S. military is getting a very sweet deal out of this. You're welcome. Now with everybody short of the president himself listening, what's the plan?"

Once again, Kendra, Andrew, and Davy repeated their strategy.

"The salvage team is already on its way from Cuba," Charley announced. "They have some ideas on how to raise the ships quickly but won't give us anything solid until after they see how the damage was created and the extent. Commander Crockett, do you have enough Chinese-speaking translators?"

"Yes, ma'am. Knowing where we were going, I pulled all but two of our Chinese-speaking SEALs from Virginia Beach. We have enough to send with each team to retake the locks and to go to the fourth ship."

"Excellent." Voices could be heard in the Pentagon room before Charley came back on the line. "You have a go."

"Capture or kill?" Commander Crockett quickly asked.

Another moment of background mumbling could be heard before she returned to the line. "We need some of the men alive on the ship in Lake Gatún. Captain Benson will be the first one through the Cocoli lock. You will then take the ship to Panama City docks where you will turn it over to the Panamanian government. Other than that, send a message to the world. No one fucks with America and its allies…and today, Panama is our ally."

The line went dead.

Andrew faced Davy. "I guess we have our answer."

"Thank Christ. I had no idea how we were going to handle all those Chinese soldiers." Davy smacked Andrew on the back. "Let's go to my office and pick your team."

CHAPTER 14

"I THINK WE'VE GOT FOUR SOLID TEAMS." ANDREW stood and stretched his arms overhead, practically touching the ceiling of Davy's office.

"I agree." Davy stood and twisted side to side. "Let's get them together and let them know what's happening." As Davy headed around his desk, his phone rang. "Crockett." He listened for a few seconds then put the phone on speaker. "Go ahead, Kendra."

"We've pieced together enough footage to guesstimate that the next change of duty will be at midnight. I'm sorry if that pushes up your timetable but everyone up here in the CIC thinks we ought to go under the cover of darkness."

Andrew and Davy glanced at their watches then at each other. A nod of confirmation and Andrew said, "We can make that happen."

"I'll get the air group commander pulling up

transports. Stay in touch." The line went dead. Andrew was beginning to wonder if anybody said *goodbye* anymore.

He followed Davy into the SEAL briefing area as everyone came to attention.

"Seats," Davy ordered and all the SEALs sat down. He called out the names of the four teams of sixteen who would be retaking the locks. "The rest of you are excused." When only sixty-four SEALs remained, Davy and Andrew briefed each team on its mission and objectives using the maps of Lake Gatún that they'd looked at in the CIC, which were now projected on the walls with enlargements of each of the four locks.

"I've purposely not introduced Commander Andrew Buchanan until now. You might recognize that name, but I'm telling you right here, right now...don't believe everything you've heard."

What the hell is Davy doing? Andrew stared at his friend, wondering what was going to come out of his mouth next.

"Zed is one of the best SEAL commanders I've ever worked with. This is the straight truth; his Trident was stolen from him. He was chosen as the scapegoat for an ugly mess that's buried so deep it will probably never see the light of day."

That was the fucking truth.

"I am as proud to serve with him today as I

was for the ten years we served side-by-side in Coronado and Virginia Beach."

Andrew wanted to throw his arms around his friend and hug him but that would be way too much. Instead, he simply said, "Thank y—"

Davy kept going. "As we all know, you have to be a SEAL in order to lead a SEAL platoon." Davy unclipped the Trident from his chest and stepped up to Andrew. "Since the CNO has ordered you to lead a SEAL team to capture a Chinese vessel, I'm interpreting that to mean he sees you as a SEAL commander. SEALs wear Tridents."

Speechless, Andrew could do nothing more than stare as his friend clipped his personal Trident onto Andrew's chest. For the first time in months, he felt whole once again. His eyes burned with unspoken emotion. The lump in his throat blocked any words, not that his mind could conjure the right thing to say.

Davy held out his hand. "Welcome back, Commander Buchanan."

Clapping and whooping filled the small room as all the SEALs came to attention and saluted. Andrew didn't have any idea how many hands he shook but being part of the brotherhood once again felt like coming home.

"Suit up, men," Davy yelled. "Meet on the flight deck in thirty minutes."

"I guess I'd better follow them since I don't have

any personal gear anymore." Andrew knew he was grinning ear to ear. "Do you think the quartermaster will have something that can fit me?"

"I'm quite sure." Davy smacked him on the shoulder.

Andrew grabbed his friend's hand once again. "Thank you."

"Don't thank me, thank the CNO." Davy turned to leave. "See you up top."

In the equipment room, the quartermaster had already pulled much of what Andrew would need. Gearing up came back to him like riding a bicycle. He'd done this thousands of times, so it was almost a mindless effort. Andrew glanced at his watch and realized he had a few minutes.

He wanted to talk to Kendra. He needed to see her. What he really wanted was to hold her. Kiss her. Tell her...what? That he had deep feelings for her?

Every time a SEAL left home, coming back was not a guarantee.

He found her in the CIC going over last-minute plans about her insertion onto the Chinese container ship. That was the perfect segue for him to take her away. "Let's go get you fitted for a harness."

As they walked out of the Command Information Center, he asked, "Have you ever fast roped?"

"Once." She looked up at him with a huge smile. "I loved it. It's a lot like zip lining."

Andrew had to agree.

When they arrived at the equipment room, it was empty. Andrew checked his watch wondering if he was already late. He still had five minutes. As he sorted through the harnesses looking for the smallest, he couldn't help commenting, "Your ex-husband is a piece of work. I understand why you divorced him."

"You don't know the half of it." There was sadness in her voice, so he stopped and took her in his arms.

"Do you want to tell me about it?"

She nodded her head as though she couldn't find the words. She swallowed hard before she spoke. "Seeing him again...being around him, brought it all back." Glistening eyes looked up at him as she fought back tears. "We were both very career minded. I wanted to wait until I was well established before we had children. Being the same rank made it hard. Our sea rotations always seemed opposite. After I commanded the destroyer in the Mediterranean, I came back ranked as the number one officer. Carter—that's his first name—had always been selected in the top five but never number one. He accused me of sleeping my way to the top."

"The bastard. He was jealous of your success, wasn't he?"

Nodding, she agreed. "I didn't see and understand that until later." She sniffed then continued. "He got selected for a one-year school and wanted me to take a desk job rather than go back out to sea. We, as in he, decided it was time to have children. So, I turned down a sea command."

She blinked several times. "I'm sure you know, anyone who wants a career in the Navy never turns down a command, least of all at sea."

"Yeah. I know." Andrew could see where this was headed.

"I ended up with a two-year desk job. As soon as he finished the year-long school, he went back to sea. He came home a few times and I visited him several times they were in port...trying to get pregnant." She choked on the word.

"I'd been tested for everything, and they couldn't figure out why I wasn't getting pregnant. Then a physician assistant suggested that Carter get tested. She looked up his records on the computer to see if anything was noted." Kendra chuckled but it wasn't humorous. "She looked at me with pity and said that she couldn't say anything because of privacy, then announced she had to leave the room. Standing, she tapped a long fingernail on the screen."

Andrew could see the answer in her eyes, but she said the words anyway. "He had a vasectomy two years after we got married." She huffed. "I also discovered he had several sexually transmitted diseases, which by the way, coincided with while I was at sea."

He shook his head side to side; it was an all too familiar story. "Is that when you divorced him?"

"Hell, yeah." Her smile was genuine. "Using my phone, I took pictures of his medical records and went straight to the JAG office to see an attorney. He was served divorce papers while in the Indian Ocean."

Kendra let out a heavy sigh. "After filing for divorce, I talked with my commanding officer who told me what I already knew; shore duty knocked me out of the promotion cycle. I was so disillusioned by then, I didn't even want to be in the same Navy with him. I considered the merchant Marines for all of ten minutes. That's an even bigger boys club than the Navy.

"I saw an ad for a cruise and decided that was an excellent place to get my head together. I took a few weeks' leave and a Caribbean cruise where I met a woman commander who showed me the bridge and talked to me about opportunities. A little research, an application, and ten days after I resigned my commission from the Navy, I joined Monarch Cruise Lines. They've been very good to me."

"Me too." Andrew kissed the top of her head. Dozens of voices came from the hall. A quick check of his watch and he had to go. Working together, they found a small enough harness and adjusted it to fit her.

"The next time I see you we'll be on the Chinese ship." He gave her a quick kiss and held her by the shoulders. "You can do this. I'll be there to catch you."

Her soft hands cupped his cheeks and pulled his face down to her. "Be safe. I have plans for you in the future." She went on tiptoes and gave him the sweetest, most tender kiss. "I'll see you on that ship."

Thirty minutes after he'd kissed Kendra goodbye, he once again jumped out of a perfectly good helicopter. From thousands of feet in the night sky, the Chinese container ship looked to be the size of a postage stamp. Landing on top of stacked boxes was going to be tricky. If he took too long to run out, he could easily fall off either into the ocean or between stacks. If he landed successfully then he and his men had to climb their way down to the ship's deck, possibly as much as eighty to a hundred feet.

Once on the main deck, they had to work their way unseen to what merchant vessels called the accommodation, where the crew lived and ate. It was underneath the bridge, which was taller than the highest container stack.

His entire platoon landed without incident and met at the designated location. Andrew went with the half of the SEALs to take the bridge while the other half systematically searched for the Chinese soldiers.

Capturing the bridge was easier than Andrew thought it would be. When he and the six highly armed men with him opened the door to the bridge, the young officer on duty fell out of the captain's chair. He'd been sleeping.

Two of the SEALs quickly restrained the only man on the bridge.

"Ask him where the soldiers are."

It took a few minutes before Chin translated.

"They are in hold number three, right in front of the machinery space. They cut an access door from the engine room into the hold then built barracks, an armory, and storage space for their food."

"Are the soldiers allowed out in the ship?" Andrew was trying to determine the danger to his other squad.

"They're not supposed to but many of them come up on deck to smoke and hang out in the machinery space."

"Fuck." Andrew paced to the edge of the windows and looked down as though he could see through the stacks of containers into the hold just below.

"They don't cook in the hold?" Andrew was trying to get an idea of the logistics. Maybe there were holes through the deck where the SEALs could drop in on them.

"No. The captain said cooking down there would be far too dangerous, so he makes them cook in the crew kitchen. They eat at different times than the crew. The kitchen runs round-the-clock to feed everybody." Chin chuckled. "He says the cooks are very unhappy and want more pay."

"No shit." Andrew then tapped his communications unit and called his other squad leader. "Cutter, tangoes are in hold number three. Access through machinery space but expect resistance."

He then switched channels so he could talk to the CIC. "I need thermal of the deck. Soldiers come up to smoke."

Less than a minute later, the command center answered, "All clear. Nothing bigger than rats."

Andrew returned to his questioning. "How many soldiers?"

"He doesn't know."

Andrew wasn't sure he believed him. With a nod from him, the two SEALs holding the young bridge officer applied pressure. The young man screamed.

"He swears he doesn't know," Chin quickly translated.

"Have him guess and tell him he'd better be damn close." Andrew wouldn't actually kill him, but he needed to put serious fear into their captive.

Seconds later he had the answer he'd expected. "About fifty."

"Ask him where the captain is," Andrew instructed Chin.

Seconds later he had his answer. "The captain is in his room, sleeping,"

The young bridge officer kept talking.

"Seems the captain got drunk after the soldiers killed the Panamanian pilot. When they had been anchored too long here in Lake Gatún, the captain of the soldiers came up the bridge. The pilot started to call his boss as soon as they showed up on the bridge with guns. The captain tried to tell the soldiers that they needed the pilot to maneuver their way to the Cocoli locks, but the soldiers shot him anyway." The translator waited for Andrew's next question.

Thoughts of their cruise ship pilot, Nigel, dashed through Andrew's mind. He swept away the image of Nigel lying dead on the bridge floor. "What did they do with the pilot's body?" He waited for his answer.

"As soon as it turned dark, they tied weights to his feet and threw his body into the water. He said the crocodiles will have eaten him by morning."

Andrew knew exactly how voracious the crocs were. He'd watched them in action. "Cowboy, find someplace to sequester all the crew. There should be about thirty of them." During the briefing, they'd considered the dining hall as an excellent facility to hold the crew hostage. Two SEALs would guard them until they reached Panama City. He named off three more of his team to start with the captain and collect the crew.

It only took his squad fifteen minutes to round up the crew and secure them in the dining area. They left all those working in the engine room. It took another half hour for the second squad to find all the Chinese soldiers and herd them into hold number three.

Andrew finally felt confident enough to call the CIC and have them send Kendra and the translator who was an expert in reading Chinese. Since she was fast roping down, they decided to have her go directly to the bridge. As soon as Andrew got the word she was in the air, he stepped out onto the roof of the accommodation, ready to catch her.

His excitement built as the sound of rotor blades filled the air. She swung out and started descending the rope.

A flash at the bow of the ship caught Andrew's eye. He knew the sound that came next. Someone had launched a rocket-propelled grenade toward the helicopter.

The chopper pilot swerved in time to miss the

grenade, but Kendra was slammed against the accommodation.

"Cutter, one tango on deck near the bow. Get that sonofabitch," Andrew called into his comm system as he ran to the other side where Kendra dangled loosely.

CHAPTER 15

"KENDRA, LOOK AT ME, DOLL."

That was Andrew's voice, but she couldn't understand his urgency. He held her in his arms, gently moving the hair off her forehead and curling it around her ear. She loved it when he did that.

"Kendra. Open up those pretty golden eyes."

No. She wanted five more minutes of sleep. Just five. She had time before she had to go on duty.

"Sir, has she been conscious at all?" What was Xia Hai doing in her bedroom with her and Andrew?

"No. Not since she hit the accommodation."

What accommodations? Did somebody need a cabin? She needed to call the hotel commander. He'd take care of it right away. What the hell was his name? Why would they need a new cabin? They were over halfway through the cruise.

She was confused. Damn. That meant she had to open her eyes and ask Andrew.

Kendra blinked several times, opening her eyes a little more with each attempt before successfully keeping them open...but she wasn't looking at the ceiling of her cabin or Andrew's. Stars glittered above her.

Andrew wasn't naked. He always slept in the nude.

She sucked in a deep breath, hoping it would clear her mind. The smell of dirty diesel assaulted her nasal passages.

Where the fuck am I?

Her left side was uncomfortable, so she shifted.

Pain shot from her shoulder to her ankle, and the fog in her brain lifted. She instantly remembered everything. She'd been fast roping out of the helicopter down to the Chinese ship, concentrating her grip pressure on the descender. She didn't want to go too fast and have an uncontrolled landing, but she couldn't dillydally dangling in air. It was hard for a pilot to hold a helicopter over one specific point.

Something had flown past her then she banged into a wall. She was obviously on the Chinese ship.

"I made it," she announced, trying to force a smile.

Andrew scooped her into his arms and held her against his rapidly rising and falling chest. He was breathing pretty hard, especially since neither of them were naked.

"Christ, doll, you scared the shit out of me." He then covered the top of her head with kisses.

"I need to get to the bridge. The SEALs have control of all three ships and the Marines have the locks. The Panamanian government is bringing in people to open and close the locks." She moved to stand up and gasped in pain, never making it vertical. Her left side wasn't cooperating. "I need to get the ship moving toward the Cocoli locks. It's going to be the first one through."

"Just lie here a minute, doll." He started gently probing her shoulder and worked his way down to her ankle. Several times she hissed when he touched a sensitive spot. He'd immediately apologized, but it still hurt like hell.

"I don't feel anything broken but you may have sprained this shoulder and ankle."

He stood carrying her in his arms as though she weighed nothing. "Let's get you on the bridge and into a chair. I also need to check your eyes to see if you have a concussion."

She put her hand on top of her head. "What happened to my helmet?"

"When you hit the side of the building, it fell off."

"Figures. It was too big but the smallest one they could find for me." With gentle fingers, she probed her scalp. "I don't feel any blood, just pain all the way down my left side."

The translator sent with her from the aircraft carrier opened the door to the empty bridge. Andrew carried her in and placed her in the captain's chair.

"Where is everybody?" Being alone in the empty bridge was almost spooky.

"The crew is in the dining hall with two of my SEALs watching them. The soldiers are down in hold number three with four SEALs watching them. The rest of my men are out looking for the asshole who shot at you."

"Is there crew in the engine room?" Kendra looked around at all the dials and gauges, glad that Xia Hai was there to translate. He was slowly making his way from the left side of the bridge to the right. "If you find the anchor motors, flip them on. Same for the diesel blowers. We need to get the ship underway."

She looked around for a minute then asked Andrew, "Where's the pilot? Usually they'll assign one who speaks the language of the captain. Hopefully he speaks English, too."

Andrew shook his head slowly side to side. "One of the Chinese officers killed him before he could call in and tell his superiors that there were armed soldiers on board."

"Shit!" Kendra didn't need to think but a minute. She pulled out her phone and called the bridge of her cruise ship. "Put Nigel on the phone."

"Who?" Lieutenant Commander Adams snidely remarked. "We don't have a Nigel on our crew."

She shook her head but stopped immediately. It hurt too much. It felt as though her brain was suspended in Jell-O. Adams was such an idiot. "The Panamanian pilot. His name is Nigel. Hand him this phone."

"Captain Benson, what can I do for you?"

"I need you over here on the Chinese container ship to guide me through to the Cocoli locks." As she moved to get more comfortable, she moaned. "How do you get on board a container ship?" Surely he wouldn't have to jump from a helicopter like her.

"There's usually a door in the mechanical space near the waterline on the port side." He continued to explain, "Somebody opens it and flips out the small steel deck. Like with your cruise ship, I jump."

Sounded simple enough as long as they could find the hatch.

Kendra spoke with Captain Phillips to arrange for a lifeboat to bring him over.

"Do you have anyone down in the engine spaces that could be pulled away long enough to open the hatch and pull Nigel in?" she asked Andrew as soon as she hung up.

"Sure," Andrew called down through his communication system. "I just need to know when he's close."

"Blowers are on. We should be ready to heat up the engines in five minutes," Xia announced. "They've been running on idle for over twenty hours according to this. By the time we get the pilot on board, the engines should be up to temperature."

Andrew came over and put his arm around Kendra. "You can do this. I have faith in you." He kissed her temple then dropped his arm. "I'm going to meet Nigel and check on my men guarding the hold. I'll be back shortly."

Xia pointed to gauges and toggle switches, helping Kendra familiarize herself with the very foreign ship. When she agreed to do this, she hadn't considered how difficult it would be because of the language barrier. Nothing was in English.

She started to get out of the chair, but the pain stopped her. "Xia, will you please look in the captain's log area for sticky notes? Maybe we can label these in English."

She and her translator were hard at work

labeling the most important gauges and switches in English when Kendra felt a breeze.

Good. Andrew is back with Nigel.

"Xia, where is the rudder control?" The translator didn't move. He simply stared toward the bridge door.

Someone spoke in Chinese, and it wasn't Xia.

Oh, fuck!

"Do we have company?" Kendra asked the translator.

"Yes. And he's standing three feet behind you pointing a gun at you."

She started to turn around and suddenly felt a cold steel barrel against the back of her head as he shouted in Chinese.

She knew the counter moves to disarm him, but she needed her whole body. With her left side barely functioning, she didn't want to take the chance.

"Stop, Captain Benson. Don't move," Xia shouted.

She inhaled a deep breath and let it out slowly, gathering her thoughts. "Ask him what he wants."

After an exchange of the Chinese singsong words, Xia replied, "He asked why you were at the helm, and I explained that the captain was drunk and being held captive in the mess hall. I told him that you were also a captain, and you could drive the ship. He wants you to take the ship to the Cocoli locks where he can complete his mission."

"I can do that. It's actually part of the plan as you well know. Tell him that's what I'm going to do." She glanced at Xia. "He doesn't need to know anything else at this point."

Xia nodded in agreement and translated.

More words were exchanged back and forth. "He wants you to free his men."

"Please tell him that I can't do that. I have no control over the American military men who have taken his soldiers hostage. My job is to maneuver the ship from here to the Pacific Coast locks."

Where the hell was Andrew? Kendra was so afraid that he and Nigel would come onto the bridge without knowing there was a Chinese soldier with a gun. How could she warn him? The soldier might shoot either one of them, or her. Her seat couldn't be seen from the entrance to the bridge.

At least she could let the gunman know that she was expecting someone. "Tell him we can't leave until Nigel is on the bridge. I need a Panamanian pilot to guide me between Lake Gatún and Cocoli locks. That area is very narrow and dangerous." Nigel had been by her side while she was driving the very small lifeboat. It was also during the daytime. She had no idea what dangers were out there for a ship this size.

Finally, the door opened again.

"Tell him not to shoot," she ordered Xia.

The translator quickly repeated the words in Chinese.

Nigel walked in. As soon as he saw the Chinese soldier holding a gun on Kendra, his eyes went huge.

"This is Nigel, the pilot," she quickly explained. "We need him to navigate all the hidden dangers between here and the locks."

The soldier grunted once Xia finished translating. She took that to mean he understood since the gun never left the back of her head.

Thirty seconds later, Andrew walked in and announced with pride, "We got him. Are we ready to go?"

Before she could say a word, the gun was gone from the back of her head and the Chinese soldier had fired at Andrew.

He fell, his bleeding head bouncing off the metal floor before it rolled to the side.

"Andrew!" Kendra screamed and flew from her chair, totally ignoring the pain shooting down her left side. She fell to her knees, carefully taking his head in her hands to see how badly he was shot.

"Xia, find the first-aid kit." Blood oozed everywhere. "Nigel, find the refrigerator and bring me water." Every bridge she'd ever been on had water for the bridge crew. Certainly, the Chinese did too.

The soldier started yelling.

"Captain Benson, he wants you to get back into the chair."

"Tell him to fuck off." Her priority was Andrew. She needed to stop the bleeding and clean the wound.

"Captain Benson," Nigel yelled. "You need to control the ship. We're drifting for land. Unless you want to ram this ship aground, you need to power the ship and turn. Now would be good."

A gentle hand touched her shoulder. Xia quietly reminded her, "You have a mission and it's not to beach this ship. It has to get to Panama City." As the director of Chinese relations at Langley, the man sure could keep his head in a volatile situation. "I'll tend to him. You save the ship."

As she was moving her hand away, her fingers brushed the communication system deep inside his ear. She deftly snatched it from Andrew. She'd never be as good at sleight-of-hand as the magician on the cruise ship, but she was proud that the Chinese gunmen didn't seem to notice.

When she stood, she almost fell back down from the pain in her ankle. Definitely not a smooth move, but it did allow her to slip the tiny comm unit into her pocket. She hobbled over to the controls, favoring her left side. She adjusted the engine speed and turned the ship away from the island.

"That should do it." She felt proud of herself… for all of a minute. She'd over-steered.

Kendra pleaded with Xia. "Tell him that I need to get the feel of how the ship handles before we head to Cocoli locks. I don't want to crash us into the steep sides of the canal. I need to make a lap around Lake Gatún."

"The soldier says no," Xia informed her as he gently cleaned the blood from Andrew's hair.

Kendra inwardly smiled. *Okay, then, we'll just see how good his sea legs are.*

"Engines ahead half, ninety degrees starboard." The ship leapt forward then lurched sideways, forcing the soldier to stumble. To his credit, he didn't fall. "Oops."

Xia translated but Kendra could hear the smile in his voice.

"Ask him again if we can make a lap around the lake. I really need to get the feel of these controls."

It took quite a bit of convincing before the Chinese soldier agreed.

For the next thirty minutes, Nigel guided her around islands in the southern part of Lake Gatún until she was able to make small and sharp movements of the huge container ship.

Every few seconds her eyes strayed from the

dials and gauges to Andrew. As far she could tell, his eyes hadn't opened.

"I think you're ready," Nigel announced. "How do you feel?"

The sooner they got to Panama City, the sooner Andrew could be treated at a hospital. Then she remembered that he could be medevac'd to the ship where an American surgeon was waiting. Probably the best time would be while going through the first set of Cocoli locks since they were currently controlled by U.S. Marines. Hopefully they'd be rid of their unwanted bridge guest by then.

"Let's do this." Kendra glanced at Andrew. He'd lost quite a bit of blood, but head wounds tended to bleed like a bitch. She needed to get him to the carrier as fast as possible. He couldn't die on her. They'd just found each other.

CHAPTER 16

"Turn to starboard and head for this open water to the east." Nigel ran his finger in a relatively straight line on the radar. After that, the canal got thin. In places, it was less than a thousand feet wide. She was thankful there wouldn't be any traffic coming from the other direction as they maneuvered down the Chagres River.

She'd captained the cruise ship into some very tight spots, but this ship was new to her and handled like she was pushing a pallet of bricks through the water. Her ship had some of the most modern navigational technology. This ship was most likely chosen because the Chinese government didn't mind scrapping it. Her father had better navigation systems on their boats thirty years ago.

With Nigel at her side, they would make it through.

"Xia, tell him that we are now headed toward the Pacific Ocean but it's going to be about four hours before we get to the Cocoli locks. We can't get there any faster with him holding a gun to the back of my head. Please, tell him it's making me nervous and I might make a mistake."

After a lengthy discussion, the Chinese soldier stepped away. He took a nearby seat facing Kendra, the gun in his lap still pointed at her.

She played with her hair around her ear several times before she dared to slip the communications unit inside. She then carefully pulled her thick brown hair over top. Kendra tapped out SOS several times then left the channel open, hoping somebody heard her call for help.

"Commander Buchanan, what the fuck are you doing?" A male voice came through her ear.

Relief washed over her like a cool shower after touring Cartagena, Columbia on a summer day. "Xia, has Commander Buchanan regained consciousness yet?"

"No. But I can tell you he's alive. His pulse is thin, and respirations are shallow." Xia said first in English then in Chinese, which seemed to placate the soldier who remained in his seat.

"Did the gunshot to his head break the skull?" Kendra hoped her questions and Xia's answers were being transmitted to the CIC.

"I can't really tell. He's still bleeding so I don't want to lift this gauze."

"Thank you, Xia, for taking care of Captain Buchanan while I navigate the ship. Is there anything else you need?" Kendra was getting worried that she hadn't heard any responses through the communication system in her ear.

The translator spoke in Chinese this time before he answered her in English. "I asked if I may have a bottle of water to drink. It seems my mouth has gone dry. The soldier said Nigel can go get one for me and should bring one to all of us."

Nigel left the radar and brought everyone a bottle of water before returning to his position. "This next maneuver is a little tricky. We didn't have to worry about it in the lifeboat, but this ship has a lot deeper draft. The channel is close to the port side. As soon as we pass between these two islands, you have to turn forty-five degrees to starboard."

Fuck. She was going to have to concentrate on the ship rather than Andrew.

She'd started into the first turn when her ex-husband's voice sounded in her ear. "Kendra, sweetheart, is it true that Commander Buchanan is injured?"

At that moment she was extremely glad that the soldier didn't speak English. "Xia, I took Andrew's communication unit and I'm now speaking with the admiral on the aircraft carrier. Once again, feel free to make up any kind of bullshit to tell the soldier with the gun pointed at me."

"Oh, Christ, sweetheart. This is exactly why I didn't want you to go on this mission. I knew you shouldn't have gone. Women should never be put in this kind of situation."

Kendra had heard the same bullshit time and time again years before. "Carter, shut the fuck up and listen. My mission is moving forward. We are passing Barro Colorado Island, still in Lake Gatún. On the bridge we have Nigel the Panamanian pilot, Xia the CIA translator, and an officer in the other army who shot Andrew in the head. He hasn't regained consciousness." Her voice broke on the last sentence.

Nigel looked at her and smiled before he spoke. "Get ready to turn forty-five degrees starboard for several minutes then we'll turn forty-five degrees again as we enter wide water for about the next fifteen to twenty minutes."

"Did you hear that?" Kendra hoped the CIC officers were following her progress.

"Copy that." It was a different male voice that responded. "We've got you."

"Did you say that you are being held at gunpoint on the bridge by a Chinese officer?" Her ex had obviously clamped down on his emotions and his tongue.

"Yes. That is the case." Kendra increased the speed as she readjusted the angle.

Xia said something to the officer in question who simply nodded. "You're doing great, Captain Benson. He has no idea what you're saying. He thinks you are talking to Nigel."

"Perfect." She let out a long slow breath.

"We'll contact the other SEALs on board and let them know the situation." That sounded like one of the CIC officers Kendra had worked with earlier that evening. "Commander Crockett is on his way back to the carrier. He might have some ideas. We'll be back in touch."

"Kendra, sweetheart. I'll get you out of there just as soon as I can." Carter was pissing her off with his familiarity and lack of respect.

"No, you won't. I have this. If you try something, you're likely to get everybody on board killed. We are proceeding with the plan. I should be there in about three and a half hours. He's not going to do anything until we are in the locks. He's determined to finish his mission. Pull your head out of your ass and think like an admiral. I am nothing more than another captain to you. Benson out."

The communications line in her head was quiet for nearly an hour. Other than the grumbling from the cheap plastic-covered seat every time she shifted positions trying to get her left side more comfortable, the bridge had been very quiet. "Captain Benson, this is Commander Crockett with the Navy SEALs."

She smiled at the new male voice. "Hey, Davy. Tell me something good."

"First, how's Andrew?"

Her report was nothing new. He'd blinked his eyes but didn't really open them. It was as though the effort put him back into a deep sleep.

"Okay, in about thirty minutes you're going to go under the Puente Centenario bridge."

"That's the bridge you stopped under, and Andrew and I went up on top to look at the locks." Nigel had expanded the radar system and pointed to the bridge they were talking about.

Kendra remembered that bridge well. The river was very narrow in that part, under one thousand feet. Fortunately, the concrete posts holding the long spans were on each side of the river.

Davy started talking in her ear once again. "As the back third passes under, keep your unwanted passenger looking forward. I'll be dropping in with some of my friends. We expect it will take us about twenty minutes to reach the bridge, but you're going to be busy maneuvering into the right side, away from the Pedro Miguel locks, heading for the Cocoli side."

"Will I be picking up the two tugboats as usual?" Kendra was quite nervous about entering the locks only under the power of the container ship since they were only one hundred feet wide and the ship she was captaining was over one hundred and eighty Kendra was quite nervous feet wide at the deck. She knew it would fit because it had come through the Agua Clara locks.

It seemed like forever before Davy came back to her. "Yes. We're going to make that happen. More of my friends will be on board the tugs along with local crew."

The news made Kendra feel a thousand times better. She glanced down at Andrew. "What's your plan for Commander Buchanan?"

Just as she had expected, as soon as the SEALs had control of the bridge, a medevac helicopter would lift him out and take him directly to the aircraft carrier where a surgeon would be ready.

"Thank you." Kendra had to concentrate because the river narrowed to five hundred feet and like all rivers, twisted and turned. As she watched her progress nearing the bridge, she worried about Davy and his team. They had to fast rope down and land on a moving ship.

She remembered from the lifeboat that there was a corner before the bridge could be seen. In the middle of the night, the tall cabling that held up the suspension bridge looked like two white triangles set side-by-side lit with huge spotlights. The bridge reflected on the river, set between rolling hills, appeared like a peaceful postcard.

"Captain Benson, we have you in sight. You'll notice that the hill on the left juts in about a hundred feet so stay to the right side of the river," Commander Crockett noted.

Kendra leaned forward and pointed out the land protrusion.

"Keep to the right side of the river," Nigel said, and Xia repeated in Chinese.

To her surprise, the soldier got out of his chair and approached the radar as though to see it for himself. She hoped he wouldn't stand there facing the stern of the ship.

He didn't move.

"Xia, tell him we'll be taking the right side of the river to start toward the Cocoli locks. He's going to want to watch this."

They started under the bridge.

"Quick. Come see." Kendra injected some excitement in her voice. "Our locks are on the right and they are all lit up." It was then she saw two black tugboats waiting at the point where ships needed to be her left to the Pedro Miguel locks, or to the right to the new wider Cocoli locks.

Xia translated but the soldier didn't move.

Kendra was ready to jump out of the chair, even though it would hurt like a bitch, and pull him to the front windows as the ship's bridge started under the Puente Centenario bridge.

The Chinese gunman walked behind Kendra and pointed the gun at the back of her head again. He spoke in his native language.

"He said your duties are almost finished." Xia spoke in English. "Because you've done as he asked, and kept your word, when the first lock is sealed behind the ship, he will allow you to get off."

"Just me?" No way in hell was that happening. She was not going to leave anyone on this bridge.

After translating, Xia nodded. "He believes I am a traitor to my country even though I explained to him I was born in the United States."

Kendra hadn't told anyone on the bridge what was going to happen. She didn't want anyone else to get up their hopes.

"Captain Benson, we are right outside the bridge door. Four of us." She recognized Davy's voice. "Where's he located?"

"I'm in the captain's chair in the middle of the bridge. He has a gun against the back of my head."

Xia said something to the Chinese gunman, supposedly translating whatever she'd said.

"Fuck! Use the bow tugboat to distract him. As soon as his attention is away from you, we'll breach the bridge."

"Nigel, Xia, we're about to get company. We have frogs on board." Kendra pointed to the first tugboat. "Tell our guest that tugboat is going to take the bow. The second one will wait until we pass by the point and take the stern. We want him to look at the tugboat."

211

Xia dutifully translated. He got up off the floor from tending to Andrew and pointed out the front windows. Although the gunman's attention moved, his gun did not.

The bridge door flung open, and four SEALs rushed in, guns up and pointed at the Chinese soldier.

Kendra bent over and put her head between her knees, completely exposing their captor. She counted two gunshots.

"He's down," somebody said in English.

A gentle hand touched her back. "Kendra, you were perfect." Davy stood between her and the corpse. "We'll get rid of that in just a minute. I need to check Andrew."

"Is there a medevac on its way?" Kendra prayed that Andrew could get help soon.

"Hovering right outside." He hand signaled to his men and two of them stepped outside. A minute later, they brought in a litter basket. Within two minutes, they had Andrew strapped in.

Kendra couldn't let him go without looking at him one more time. She might never see him again. She slid out of the chair and put a hand on one of the SEALs arm. Gazing down at him, his skin was so pale. His head wrapped in a cushioned helmet and blankets were tucked all around him.

Kendra bent down next to his ear. "I couldn't let you go without telling you…"

She swallowed hard and kissed his exposed cheek. "I love you. Don't you dare die on me." She whispered the words, not truly caring if anyone else heard them, just praying that it was true that a patient in a coma could hear and understand what people said to him.

She stood quickly because she wanted him to get to surgery or whatever he needed as soon as possible.

When the door opened, she could hear the spinning rotors.

Davy came up and put his arm around her shoulders. "I take it you two are a thing?"

Kendra shrugged and told the truth, "I don't know what we are."

"Captain Benson, the second tugboat is about to engage." Nigel gazed at her with sad eyes. "I'm sorry, but we need you at the helm."

Nodding, Kendra resumed her position in the captain's chair.

"You've got this." Davy patted her shoulder. "I'm going to check on all the other SEALs and reestablish communication with them as officer in charge. I'll be back if you need me." He tapped his ear. "Just call."

CHAPTER 17

"Excellent job!" Nigel smiled at Kendra.

She'd exited the third Cocoli lock and expertly zigzagged the huge container ship toward the Pacific Ocean. The CIC directed her to the pier where the Panamanian government officials met her and took possession of the ship. She was thanked by everyone from the U.S. ambassador's representative to someone from the Panamanian president's office. She simply went through the motions, too exhausted from everything she'd gone through in the past twenty-four hours; being slammed against a building, captaining a strange ship, Andrew being shot, being held captive at gunpoint, and finally being allowed to leave the Chinese container ship.

The officials were followed on board by dozens of Panamanian soldiers. The Chinese soldiers were marched off the ship in handcuffs, soon followed by the SEALs, tired but joking.

Davy entered the bridge as she watched her cruise ship pass by. "You will be back on board soon. CIC just told me that your ship is docking at cruise port on Perico Island. It's not scheduled to leave until nine o'clock tonight."

Kendra grabbed her phone and called Captain Phillips. Davy's information had been correct. Everyone who had an excursion booked would take it from Panama City. Monarch Cruise Lines had arranged to take everyone on board to San Diego. Since they were going to miss two ports in the Caribbean on their way back to Miami, Puerto Vallarta and Cabo San Lucas had been added to the schedule.

Although she'd only been gone from the cruise ship eighteen hours, it felt like months. She was exhausted from the tension of captaining an unfamiliar ship all through the night, and worrying about Andrew.

"Ready to go?" Davy asked. "There's a military Jeep waiting for you at the end of the wharf. It'll take you back to your ship."

"Let's just say I'm ready to get off this ship." She touched Davy's forearm. "I'd really like to go to the aircraft carrier and see how Andrew is doing." For the last two hours she'd been living moment to moment on the premise that no news was good news, not that they had any reason to notify her one way or the other. She wasn't family.

"I don't think that's in the cards, but you might have better luck with the admiral than anyone else." Davy held open the bridge door as they started descending several stories so they could exit through the engine room at the dock line.

"I'm definitely not his favorite person right now." Kendra thought about her last words to her ex-husband. If other people had been listening, and surely they were, she'd embarrassed him. He wouldn't even consider granting her any favors. No. They were a thing of the past. She'd torched that bridge.

As they walked down the pier, the orange streaks of a new dawn peeked over the mountains of Soberania National Park that separated the two oceans. By the time they reached the military vehicle, half the sun could be seen over the mountain tops.

Davy had been in constant contact with his men and the CIC, so Kendra enjoyed watching the sunrise, ignoring his constant dialogue. With his hand on the door to the Jeep, he held up one finger while finishing his conversation.

"You'll be very happy to know that Andrew did not need surgery. But he does have one hell of a headache."

"Oh, my God, that's the best news I've heard today." Kendra wanted to jump up and down, but she simply didn't have the energy.

"The bullet burned a gouge in his hair and scraped that hard head of his, but it didn't penetrate. Didn't even crack it. The impact of the bullet, though, knocked him out. Falling on the floor and having his head bounce on the steel added insult to injury. The doctor wants to keep him a few more hours but plans to release him before we head all the way around South America."

"I take it the salvage team couldn't raise the other container ship out of Agua Clara?" Kendra leaned against the vehicle and crossed her arms and ankles.

"They haven't arrived yet. Admiral Ward has made the decision that the fleet needs to get to the Pacific Ocean as fast as possible." Davy leaned beside her. "Marines are on their way from Camp Lejeune and Camp Pendleton to take over guarding the locks until the Panamanian forces are on site."

He stared at her for a long moment. "Andrew is the best man I know. Most men would be bitter after what happened to him."

"What did happen?" She didn't know what he was talking about.

Davy shook his head. "That's not for me to say. I'm sorry I even brought it up."

She looked toward the mountains as the sun fully emerged over the edge. "Neither of us mentioned our previous Navy life. When we got together, it was like a new beginning for both of us." She released a heavy sigh. "He now knows why I left the Navy. Maybe someday he'll feel confident enough to tell me why he did."

"Do you love him?" The abrupt change of subject forced her gaze to Davy.

"Yes. I think I do. Hell, I don't know." She turned toward him. "I'm just not sure how we would make it work. Would they reinstate him as a Navy SEAL? He also has the opportunity to join a group of former SEALs called the Holt Agency. I have no idea what decision he'll make."

"My wife is in international banking. Like me, she travels a lot. We make it work because we love each other. Don't give up on him. Love is worth it." Davy stood up and opened the vehicle door. "We couldn't have done this without you. Thank you."

"The next time you and your wife are stateside, look me up. I'd love for you to take a cruise on my ship." She slid onto the seat and leaned out the open window. "I'm serious."

Davy's smile was soft as though he was thinking about his wife. He nodded. "Angela would love that. And it would be nice to be on the ocean in something other than a big gray ship." He tapped the roof twice, signaling the driver to go. "I'll call you."

ANDREW FINISHED the bowl of soup as Davy walked into his room at sick bay. "Thanks for getting me here so soon."

"Don't thank me, thank Kendra. She got your comm unit and got word to us that you were hurt." Davy raised one eyebrow. "And it took several hours."

"Seemed like minutes to me." Andrew didn't remember anything after walking onto the bridge. When he woke up, the nurse had told him he'd been shot in the head.

"Asshole, you were unconscious."

"Damn. So it was Kendra that saved me." He'd be sure to thank her as soon as he saw her. Maybe he'd show her just how thankful he was.

"She's one hell of a woman. You'd be a fool if you let that one get away."

Andrew puffed up his chest. "Yeah. I know. We're going to spend some time together at my beach house in Miami once she's finished with this contract."

"You'd better lock her down sooner rather than later." Davy was right.

"I will, just as soon as they let me out of here."

Twelve hours later, Andrew walked up the

gangplank back onto his cruise ship. Still dressed in all black, blood staining much of his shirt, white gauze wrapped around his head, he knew he was a shock to his security team.

"I'll be on light duty for couple days." Although everyone wanted to hear about his adventure, he slowly shook his head side to side and promised, "I'll tell you what I can tomorrow. Right now, I need a shower and some clean clothes." He also had to report in to Captain Phillips so his second-in-command could continue as security officer.

Captain Phillips followed him off the bridge, out of hearing distance. "Captain Benson isn't to report to duty until tomorrow morning. I think she's been asleep since she returned early this morning." He grinned. "You might want to order up some food for both of you. I'll see you in the morning as well."

Andrew desperately needed a shower before he knocked on Kendra's door. After ordering all her favorites, and several of his, he stepped into wet hot bliss. Clean clothes felt heavenly, especially since they were some of his softest civilian jeans and a T-shirt.

When the food arrived, delivered personally by the commander of food and beverage, Andrew slid into a pair of flip-flops. He'd forgotten just how uncomfortable boots were after twelve hours.

"I don't know what part you had in opening the canal but thank you." The man set down the heavy tray. "We were told Captain Benson was at the helm of the carrier ship that went through just before us. Is it true?"

Andrew didn't see any reason to lie. Most of the truth would come out eventually. "Yes." He'd let her decide if she was going to tell anyone on board the cruise ship about being held captive at gunpoint.

The commander headed back toward the door. "Tell her we are all so very proud of her."

If they only knew the half of it, they'd never look at her the same again.

Andrew picked up the tray and followed him out the door, knocking on hers. She answered with sleepy eyes that went wide when she saw him.

Grabbing the tray, she headed for her small dining table yelling over her shoulder, "Get in here." As soon as she set it down, she threw herself at him. "I was so afraid..."

He held her close, pulling her head to his chest. This was where she belonged. Right here. Forever. Davy's words dashed through his mind. But he needed to reassure her first. "I'll be fine. A little light duty for a day or two." She leaned back and he saw those gorgeous golden eyes. "Captain Phillips said we both have off until tomorrow morning."

She grinned up at him. "So light duty means I'm on top."

Later that night, after round two, they were lying in her bed, naked in each other's arms. "Doll, I love just lying here, holding you like this."

She rolled her head and looked up at him. "Me too."

You'd better lock her down sooner rather than later. Davy's words settled in the back of his mind.

He pulled her even closer while staring into her beautiful eyes. "I love you, Kendra. And this is where I want you forever."

She rolled on top of him and cupped his cheeks with her hands. "I love you too." Her kiss was tentative. "I'm just not sure how this can work out."

He lifted his knees, spreading her legs. "I think it works out just fine." He slid his erection into her already slick heat. "I love you...and you love me, right?"

"Oh, yes." She bent and took his mouth; this time the kiss was filled with love and passion.

"And you're coming to Miami as soon as your contract is finished, right?" He drove up into her as she came down on his shaft.

"Yes." She panted the word as all the muscles in her body tightened.

"We're good now, right?" He moved his thumb

to circle her clit, forcing her over the edge. He followed her over they fell asleep once again.

He woke with her gently touching the edge of the gauze that wrapped around his head. When he opened his eyes, all he could see was her face peering down at him.

"I love you. I tried like hell not to fall in love with you, but you stole my heart, step-by-step as we ran the track in the mornings." She smiled, then giggled. "And ounce by ounce with the chocolate decadence that you brought me after a hard day." She bent and gave him a quick peck on the lips.

"Were you afraid to fall in love again?" There was no way in hell he wanted to bring her ex into their bed, but he needed to know.

"No. I was afraid to fall in love with someone in the same profession again."

He gave her a huge smile. "Good thing we're not the same profession. I have no desire to drive a ship. I kinda like this security officer gig." He reconsidered for all of a second. "Most of the time." He pulled her in closer. "Let's not do the part where you get taken hostage ever again, okay?"

"I'd prefer to never be held at gunpoint again." Her face turned serious. "But if I am, you're the only man I want by my side."

"I'm the only man who had better be by your

side." He kissed her long and hard. "I'm talking forever, doll."

"You hadn't better be asking me to marry you while were naked in bed together," she warned.

"Of course not." Although he had been, kind of. He'd certainly been trying to, as Davy said, lock her down. "I'll find the perfect place and surprise you." Right after he bought a ring.

EPILOGUE

"I can't believe Monarch ended my contract when we got to San Diego." Kendra dug her toes into the warm sand on Miami Beach.

"You were awarded so many fucking accolades from the U.S. Navy, the United States government and Panamanians, they couldn't keep you on as staff captain." He rolled over on the blanket and kissed her. "Are you complaining that you got to start your two-month vacation early?"

"Hell, no. I'm just sorry it's almost over." She sighed. "We've only got two more weeks to enjoy this beautiful beach."

Andrew looked at his watch. "Actually, doll, we only have one more day."

"What? We rented it for a whole month more." He loved it when she got riled up.

"I only extended our lease two weeks," he

confessed. Then grinned at her. "I've made a few other plans." He made a point of looking at his watch once again. "We should probably go in and pack. We're going on a Caribbean cruise."

"Please don't tell me were going back to the Panama Canal." She dramatically shivered. "I'm not sure I could go there yet, even though it's open again."

"No. I think we'll be avoiding that destination cruise for a while." He stood and pulled her up. "It's not even a Monarch Cruise." She shook out the blanket as he collected the umbrella and cooler. "We're on vacation. I don't want anyone to even recognize us."

Along with the thousands of other guests, Kendra and Andrew walked onto one of the largest cruise ships currently sailing. He liked being just another couple to enjoy a week in the Caribbean, taking excursions at every port, eating any time their little hearts desired. As they walked across the Lido deck later that afternoon, Kendra shrieked and let go of his hand. He watched her run to the master of the ship, then signal him to join them.

"Andrew, I want you to meet Captain Tomusko. She's the reason I'll get my own ship in a few weeks. A decade ago, when I was feeling my lowest, she introduced me to my new career."

"Very nice to meet you, Commander," she said as they shook hands. "I'm sure I'll be seeing more of you." She stepped back. "If you two will excuse me, I have a ship to cast off. Please join me for supper. We'll catch up then."

Late that night, after watching a beautiful Caribbean sunset and eating decadent chocolate after the show, Andrew and Kendra walked hand-in-hand. They stopped at the bow of the ship, smelling the ocean air as the breeze lifted Kendra's dark brown hair.

"I've always loved the ship at night," Kendra said as she lifted her hair to the wind allowing it to flow, cooling her scalp, rather than drape onto her shoulders. After letting it grow for several months, she was realizing how heavy it was in the steamy Caribbean.

"The stars are my favorite. You can see so many more when at sea." He looked up, knowing she would follow his gaze. He then dropped to one knee. "Kendra Benson..."

She looked down to where his face normally was then looked down to the deck. "Oh, my God," she squealed.

He started again. "Kendra Benson, would you make me the happiest man on this earth and marry me?"

"Yes." She then pulled him up and threw her arms around him. "Yes." Kiss. "Yes." Kiss. "Yes." Followed by the longest kiss.

"Good. Because I don't want to wait." He nodded at the captain who came forward.

"Oh, my God. We're doing this? Now?"

Andrew shrugged. "Sure, why not."

"And what did we decide about witnesses?" the captain asked. "We're required to have two."

Kendra laughed out loud. "What the hell. Invite everybody."

"Ladies and gentlemen," the captain announced through the microphone. "If you would like to join Captain Kendra Benson and Commander Andrew Buchanan as I unite them in holy matrimony in a midnight wedding on the bow, please join us now."

Hundreds of guests who were enjoying their first night at sea lined the railing for the most unique wedding they'd ever see.

Two weeks later, Kendra and Andrew kissed for the hundredth time on the pier in Miami. Next to them stood a premier class cruise ship, which Kendra would take over as master...as soon as they quit kissing.

"I'll see you soon." Andrew gave her one last kiss then turned her around and smacked her butt. "Be safe, my love."

He watched her walk up the gangplank and be saluted by her new crew and staff.

He hid in the shadows and chuckled. He gave her half an hour before boarding his new cruise ship, meeting first with the staff captain then his new security team. He stayed busy until they were underway, as usual. Kendra had texted him several times with pictures of her new bridge and crew. He'd made appropriate comments and wished her well.

Andrew took the stairs to the bridge and allowed her staff captain to introduce him along with the rest of her staff. "Ma'am, I'd like to introduce you to Commander Buchanan, your new security officer."

Kendra threw herself into his arms. "You sonofabitch." Their kiss was short as she slid back out of his arms. "Ladies and gentlemen, I'd like to introduce you to my husband, Commander Andrew Buchanan." She punched him in the arm. "At least this time we won't have to hide from the captain."

THE END

SNEAK PEEK

If you've enjoyed reading *Shadow in the Daylight* by KaLyn Cooper, please consider reading the next book in the Shadow SEALS Series, *Shadow in the Darkness* by Becca Jameson.

Here's a sneak peek!

Shadow in the Darkness / Chapter One

"Is all this VIP treatment really necessary?" Grant muttered under his breath as he and his friends reached the front of the receiving line to board the cruise ship. The fanfare seemed over the top.

As he walked down the short line, each officer offered assurances that Grant should contact them personally if he needed anything pertaining to their responsibilities. *Right, like I'd contact a commander if I need more towels.* His Navy training would never allow that.

"Welcome aboard." The dark-haired woman with the big smile held out a hand in greeting.

Quickly counting the gold stripes on her cuff, he realized she was a captain. With a glance at her name-tag that read Kendra Benson, he shook her hand. "It's a pleasure to be aboard your ship, Captain Benson."

"She smiled. "You must be Andrew Buchanan's friends."

"Yes, ma'am, we are."

"As our ship's security officer, Andrew's busy right now but asked me to personally greet you."

"Ah." Grant smiled. "Well, thank you. That wasn't necessary. We didn't expect him to be able to be here waiting for us. I'm sure there are a million things on his plate before departure later this afternoon."

"Indeed." Kendra shook the hands of the rest of Grant's friends: Tavis, Keene, and Holden. All of them former SEALs. All of them recently hired by the Holt Agency, which didn't officially open for business for another few weeks.

Thus, the much-needed vacation before they started their new careers.

"I believe Andrew is going to give you a tour of the ship," Kendra leaned in and said quietly so none of the other passengers heard. "We don't do behind the scenes tours anymore, but Andrew thought you'd be interested."

"That would be cool," Holden stated. "We're overly familiar with a lot of ships, but none of them have been cruise ships." He chuckled as he adjusted the strap of his backpack on his shoulder.

"Well, you'll find that you don't have to duck your heads on this ship," Kendra joked. "Nor will you be bunking with dozens of people in stacked bunkbeds."

Grant laughed. "That's good to know. We'd also like to request as little drama as possible if you can arrange it," he teased. "We're not in the mood for pirates or enemy ships." He shuddered.

"Enemy ships are incredibly unlikely." She leaned in once again and whispered, "Pirates do happen from time to time, but not often while touring the Caribbean and the Panama Canal. The Suez Canal, that's a different story."

"Can we not even joke about pirates and enemy ships right now?" Keene shuddered.

Kendra stood straight, squared her shoulders, and spoke so everyone in line could hear her. "None of that is in the plan. Just a relaxing eleven-day cruise. Four ports including the canal. Sunshine. Evening entertainment. All the food you can eat. I promise the mess halls on this ship have much better food than a military ship."

Tavis nodded agreement. "I need a beer and a burger."

When her phone buzzed, she excused herself and took a step back. Her face turned soft with a small smile. She quickly rejoined the four men. "Both of those can be arranged. As soon as you get to your cabin, call room service and place the order. You can enjoy the burger while you get settled and knock that first beer back. Andrew will meet you back here in an hour for a tour. How does that sound?"

"Excellent," Grant agreed. He was really looking forward to that beer, but he did want to tour the ship and see his good friend, Andrew.

Andrew was the one who had arranged for the four of them come aboard for this vacation. It was his last voyage before he might be moving on to his next career. He too had been asked to join the rest of them working for the Holt Agency in a few months.

Even though Andrew would be extremely busy during the cruise, hopefully he would get to spend some time with the rest of the guys on his days off. It was an opportunity for Grant and the others to get some R&R.

All four men had been through hell lately. The other three men had recently endured capture and torture that had involved attempted government coverups that ended their careers. Didn't matter that none of them were at fault. Medical retirement had been their best option, especially for the politicians involved. Grant's story was no less heroic, and Andrew's was enough to piss off the Pope.

It had been an easy decision for Grant after he'd taken the call from Ajax Cassman and Ryker Tufano. The two of them had been in Ethiopia when the rest of their team had been captured and held hostage. Among those hostages were Holden, Keene, and Tavis.

Grant had found himself in a similar situation in Brazil not long after the first incident. He'd been presumed dead and left behind in the Amazon. Intentionally. With no evidence or proof. Lucky for him, he'd managed to survive a month in the jungle, finally making his way to civilization only to find out no one had been looking for him.

It burned every time Grant thought about it. Those who were responsible were now behind bars. Grant had been given several options and chose to leave the military for good. That had been when he'd gotten a call from Ajax and Ryker who'd invited him to come to Indiana for a business proposition.

That had also been when Grant's life changed course for the better.

In a few weeks, he would be employed full-time by the Holt Agency. He would no longer work directly for the government. From now on, he would be in the private sector. Most of the clients the Holt Agency anticipated would come from the U.S. government though. There were plenty of jobs the government didn't want to get involved in. Jobs that were either too dirty, too dangerous, or too secretive.

The pay would be fantastic. Sure, Grant might have to travel a lot, often out of the country, but if a job didn't suit his schedule, he could turn it down. Let someone else take it. A win-win. Sounded like his dream job.

All of the adventure and excitement with none of the bureaucratic shit he'd dealt with for so many years.

And the best part? Regular vacations, like this one he was about to enjoy before he even started working. He was taking this trip with three other guys who would also be working for the Holt Agency when it officially opened.

Technically, all four of them were already on the payroll. The Holt Agency wasn't advertising its services yet, but word had gotten out. It was possible Grant could end up with an assignment before the agency was officially open for business. But he didn't need to worry about that today. Not for the next eleven days.

He was in vacation mode for the first time he could remember. Sure, he had his phone in his pocket. They all did. But there were plenty of other guys on the new team who weren't on vacation and would be much higher up the list in the event someone was needed for a job.

Not Grant. Not Holden, Keene, or Tavis.

Holden clasped Grant's arm. "Let's go find our cabins and call room service. We can change into casual clothes before we start the tour."

Keene nodded. "Sounds like a plan."

"I am pretty excited to get a tour of the ship

though," Tavis pointed out. "I hope we get some behind-the-scenes treatment."

"I'm sure we will." Grant nodded.

"No need to go hunting your cabin." Captain Benson nodded toward the twenty-something woman to her right. "Gentlemen, Ms. Neely will escort you to your cabins. It's all part of our VIP service."

Holden stepped up to the shapely young lady and held out his hand. "My name is Holden Billings, and you are…?"

Order *Shadow in the Darkness*
Shadow SEALs Series
by Becca Jameson
Releasing 9/12/2022

Thank you for reading the Shadow SEALS series by the Shadow Sisters!

BOOKS IN THE SHADOW SEALS SERIES

I hope you enjoyed reading *Shadow in the Mountains* as much as I enjoyed writing it! Here's a complete list of all the books in the Shadow SEALs series

- First Season:

June 8, 2021 Cat Johnson *Shadow Pawn*
June 29, 2021 Elle James *Shadow Assassin*
July 20, 2021 Becca Jameson *Shadow in the Desert*
Aug 10, 2021 KaLyn Cooper *Shadow in the Mountain*
Aug 31, 2021 Donna Michaels *Shadow of a Chance*
Sept 21, 2021 J.M. Madden *Shadow of the Moon*
Oct 12, 2021 Sharon Hamilton *Shadow of the Heart*
Jan 4, 2022 Desiree Holt *Shadow Defender*
Jan 25, 2022 Elaine Levine *Not My Shadow*
Feb 15, 2022 Abbie Zanders *Cast in Shadow*

- Second Season:

March 8, 2022 Cat Johnson *Shadow Lies*
April 12, 2022 Donna Michaels *Shadow of Hope*
June 21, 2022 J.M. Madden *Shadow Games*
July 12, 2022 Sharon Hamilton *Shadow Warrior*
Aug 23, 2022 KaLyn Cooper *Shadow in the Daylight*
Sept 13, 2022 Becca Jameson *Shadow in the Darkness*

ABOUT THE AUTHOR

KaLyn Cooper is a USA Today Bestselling author whose romances blend fact and fiction with blazing heat and heart-pounding suspense. Life as a military wife has shown KaLyn the world, and thirty years in PR taught her that fact can be stranger than fiction. She leaves it up to the reader to separate truth from imagination. She, her husband, and Little Bear (Alaskan Malamute) live in Tennessee on a micro-plantation filled with gardens, cattle, and quail. When she's not writing, she's at the shooting range or paddling on the river.

For the latest on works in progress and future releases, check out
KaLyn Cooper's website www.KaLyn-Cooper.com
http://www.kalyncooper.com/

Follow **KaLyn Cooper on Facebook** for promotions and giveaways
https://www.facebook.com/KaLynCooper1Author/

Sign up for exclusive promotions and special offers only available in **KaLyn's newsletter** https://kalyncooper.com/kalyn-cooper-newsletter

MORE BOOKS BY KALYN COOPER

Black Swan Series

MILITARY ACTIVE DUTY WOMEN SECRETLY TRAINED in Special Operations and the men who dare to capture the heart of a Woman Warrior.

Unconventional Beginnings Prequel (Black Swan novella #0.5) ~ He's dead. But they can't allow it to affect her. She's too important. Download FREE
https://dl.bookfunnel.com/uec4utb66d

Unrelenting Love: Lady Hawk (Katlin) & Alex (Black Swan novel #1) ~ Women in special operations? Never… Until he sleeps with the most lethal woman in the world.

Noel's Puppy Power: Bailey & Tanner (A Sweet

Christmas Black Swan novella #1.5) ~ He's better at communicating with animals than women, but as an amputee she knows firsthand it's the internal scars that can be most difficult to heal.

Uncaged Love: Harper & Rafe (Black Swan novel #2) ~ The jungle isn't the only thing that's hot while escaping from a Colombian cartel.

Unexpected Love: Lady Eagle (Grace) & Griffin (Black Swan novel #3) ~ He never believed in love, but he never expected to find her.

Challenging Love: Katlin & Alex (A Black Swan novella #3.5) ~ A new relationship can be fragile when outsiders are determined to challenge that love.

Unguarded Love: Lady Harrier (Nita) & Daniel (Black Swan novel #4) ~ She couldn't lose another sick baby...then he brought her his dying daughter.

Choosing Love: Grace & Griffin (A Black Swan novella #4.5) ~ Hard choices have to be made when parents interfere in a growing relationship.

Unbeatable Love: Lady Falcon (Tori) & Marcus (Black Swan novel #5) ~ Scarred outside and in, why would his beautiful friend ever want more with him?

Unmatched Love: Lady Kite (Lei Lu) & Henry (Black Swan novel #6) ~ Scarred outside and in, why would his beautiful friend ever want more with him?

Unending Love: Lady Falcon (Tori) & Marcus (Black Swan novel #7) ~ Their life together is not over. He has to believe it…or it will be.

Guardian ELITE Series

FORMER SPECIAL OPERATORS, these men work for Guardian Security (from the Black Swan Series) protecting families in their homes and executives on the road, but they can't always protect their hearts.

ELITE Redemption (Guardian ELITE Book 1) ~ Guarding a billionaire and his wife isn't easy when you can't keep your eyes off your bikini wearing, gun carrying partner who is lethal in stilettos. *This book was previously published as **Double Jeopardy**.*

ELITE Justice (Guardian ELITE Book 2) ~ She's

not what she seems. Neither is he. But the terrorist threat is real. So is the desire that smolders between them. *This book was previously published as **Justice for Gwen**.*

ELITE Rescue (Guardian ELITE Book 3) ~ When Jacin awoke stateside, he remembered nothing about his escape from the Colombian cartel or his torture. He was sure of only one thing, his love of Melina, his handler. When she disappears, neither bruises nor the CIA will keep him from rescuing her. *This book was previously published as Rescuing Melina.*

ELITE Protection (Guardian ELITE Book 4) ~ Terrorists want her...but so does he. The chase isn't the only thing that heats up when the flint of the former SEAL strikes against the steel of the woman warrior. *This book was previously published as Snow SEAL.*

ELITE Defense (Guardian ELITE Book 5) ~ Guarding her wasn't his job, but he couldn't let her die...even before she stole his heart. When he discovers the temptingly beautiful foreign service officer is being threatened, his protective instincts take over. *This book was previously published as Securing Willow.*

ELITE Damnit (Guardian ELITE Book 6) ~ With

a hurricane bearing down on the tiny island, they only have days to find and rescue ten kidnapped young girls and their chaperones…and keep their hands off each other. *This book was previously published as a short story titled Damnit I Love You.*

Suspense Sisters

THE SHADOW SEALs were once the best of the best, recruited from obscurity after their fall from grace to work in the shadows, enacting justice upon our enemies and protecting those caught in the crosshairs by any means necessary.

Shadow in the Mountain Another mission into the shadows was the last place he wanted to be. Last time it ended his career. This time promises death or salvation.

Shadow in the Daylight After he left the SEALs, Andrew did a covert job for Charley before parting ways. As the Security Officer aboard a cruise ship, he invited several SEAL friends to travel as his guests through the Panama Canal. He never imagined he'd need their highly trained skills.

Cancun Series

FOLLOW THE GIRARD FAMILY —along with their friends, former SEALs and active duty female Navy pilots—as they hunt Mayan antiquities, terrorists and Mexican cartels in what most would call paradise. Tropical nights aren't the only thing HOT in Cancun.

Christmas in Cancun (Cancun Series Book #1) ~ Can the former SEAL keep his libido in check and his family safe when the quest for ancient Mayan idols turns murderous?

Conquered in Cancun (Cancun Series Novella #1.5) ~ A helicopter pilot's second chance at love walks into a Cancun nightclub, but she's a jet fighter pilot with reinforced walls around her heart.

Captivated in Cancun (Cancun Series Book #2) ~ His job is tracking down terrorists so he's not interested in a family. She wants him short-term, then needs him when their worlds collide.

Claimed by a SEAL (Cancun Series crossover Novella #2.5 with Cat Johnson's Hot SEALs) ~ How far will the Homeland Security agent go to assure mission success when forced undercover for a second time with an irresistible SEAL?

Never Forgotten Trilogy

THE MISSION BROUGHT the five of them together, disaster nearly tore them apart, a mystery and killer reunited them forever.

A Love Never Forgotten (Never Forgotten novel #1) ~ Dreams or nightmares. Truth or lies. He can't tell them apart. Then he discovers the woman who has haunted his dreams is real. Is she his future? Or his past?

A Promise Never Forgotten (Never Forgotten novel #2) ~ As a Marine Lieutenant Colonel, he could take on any mission and succeed. Raising his two godchildren…with her…just might kill him.

A Moment Never Forgotten (Never Forgotten novel #3) ~ The moment he realized she was in serious danger…he couldn't protect her.